Mary Elizabeth Braddon, Mary Elizabeth Braddon

An Open Verdict

Vol. 2

Mary Elizabeth Braddon, Mary Elizabeth Braddon

An Open Verdict
Vol. 2

ISBN/EAN: 9783337050177

Printed in Europe, USA, Canada, Australia, Japan

Cover: Foto ©Andreas Hilbeck / pixelio.de

More available books at **www.hansebooks.com**

AN OPEN VERDICT

A Novel

BY THE AUTHOR OF

'LADY AUDLEY'S SECRET'

ETC. ETC. ETC.

IN THREE VOLUMES

VOL. II.

LONDON:

JOHN MAXWELL AND CO.

4, SHOE LANE, FLEET STREET.

1873

AN OPEN VERDICT.

CHAPTER I.

'DEATH BRINGS COOL NIGHT AFTER LIFE'S SULTRY DAY.'

MONDAY morning was bleak and cold. There was neither frost nor snow, but a driving rain that beat fiercely upon all the southern windows of the Water House, and obscured the view of river and village, church tower and moorland.

At nine o'clock Beatrix was still sleeping. Bella, to whom necessity had given the habit of early rising, was dressed and out of her room before eight, and found herself at a loss for occupation. There was a cheery fire in Miss Harefield's sitting-room, and the breakfast was laid—a snug round table bright with pretty china and quaint old silver, with an old blue and red Oriental bowl of hothouse flowers in the centre. How different from the Scratchell table, with its tumbled week-old cloth, which was like an enlarged copy of Mercator's Chart of the World, done in tea and coffee—its odds and ends of crockery, all cracked—for what pottery that ever the potter moulded could withstand the destructiveness of the young Scratchells?—the battered old Britannia teapot, stale quartern loaf, scanty remnant of salt butter, and inadequate dish of pale-faced rashers, the distribution of which half-cured pig gave rise to much ill-will and recrimination among Mr. Scratchell's olive branches!

At home Bella would have had to help in the preparation of the morning meal, and to assist her overworked mother in the struggle to preserve peace and order while it was being eaten. Here she had nothing to do but to sit and watch the logs burning, and listen to the clock ticking and the rain lashing the windows, while she waited for Beatrix.

This state of existence, placid though it was

as compared with the turmoil of home, soon began to pall upon Bella, who was of an essentially active temper. She went to the window and looked out, but could see only dim shapes of mountain and moor through the blinding rain. She thought of Cyril Culverhouse, who was going his rounds already, perhaps, in the cold and rain, or teaching damp children in a windy schoolroom. She thought of her poor mother, whose much-tried spirit was doubtless being exercised by the tea-kettle's obstinate persistence in not boiling, and of her father, who was most likely making himself an affliction to everybody with his well-known Monday morning temper.

To-morrow would be Christmas Day. This afternoon Miss Harefield's presents, and Bella's poor little offerings were to be sent to the Scratchells. Bella wondered whether her father would be molli-fied in temper as evening wore round so far as to allow of egg-flip or snapdragon—those luxuries for which the young Scratchells always pleaded, but wherewith they were but seldom gratified. Yet, by and by, when going down the hill of life, they would look back fondly upon this arid childhood, and, softened by distance, the rare and scanty pleasures of these early days would seem to them sweeter than anything which a prosperous later life could yield.

The clock struck the quarter after nine, and still Bella sat looking at the fire, with the breakfast table undisturbed. Even the urn had left off hissing. Beatrix was not generally so late. The two girls had been accustomed to sit down together at eight, for in Miss Scales' moral code late hours were sinful, and a nine o'clock breakfast was the first stage in a downward career.

Bella's patience was exhausted. She went to Beatrix's door and knocked. No answer. She knocked louder, and called, and still there was no answer. She was beginning to feel uneasy, when she saw the young woman who waited on Miss Harefield coming along the corridor.

'Is your mistress up, Mary? Have you done her hair?'

'No, miss. I went at half-past seven, as usual, but she was sleeping so sound I didn't like to wake her. I know she has had bad nights lately, and I thought the sleep would do her good. I've been on the listen for her bell ever since.'

' And she has not rung ?'

' No, miss.'

Bella went in without another word. Beatrix was sleeping profoundly.

' Don't wake her, miss,' said the maid, looking in at the door. ' She's been wanting sleep all along. Mr. Namby says so. Let her have her sleep out.'

' Very well,' assented Bella. ' I'll go and have my breakfast. I'm quite exhausted with waiting.'

' So you must be, miss, and the urn is cold and the eggs too, I'll lay. I'll go and get things hotted up for you.'

Bella sat down to her lonely breakfast, presently, profound silence reigning in the house, and a dulness as of the grave. She began to think that, after all, wealth was not an unqualified blessing. Here was the heiress to one of the finest estates in Yorkshire, with innumerable acres in Lincolnshire to boot, leading an existence so joyless and monotonous that even one week of it was too much for Miss Scratchell. And yonder at the Park the wife of a millionaire was hastening her descent to the grave by vain cares and needless economies. The rich people did not seem, according to Bella's small experience, to get value for their money.

She was still sitting at breakfast when she was surprised by a visit from the butler.

'Oh, if you please, ma'am,' he began, with a serious air, 'Mrs. Peters and I are rather anxious about Mr. Harefield. We really don't feel to know what we ought to do—the circumstances are altogether out of the way. I don't want to do more than my duty as a faithful servant—and I shouldn't feel satisfied if I was to do less.'

'But what is wrong?' asked Bella, puzzled and scared by this circumlocution, and now perceiving the round rubicund visage of the housekeeper looking in at the door. 'Is Mr. Harefield ill?'

'No, Miss Scratchell, it isn't that—but we cannot find him.'

'You can't find him?'

'No, ma'am. He isn't in his bedroom, and

what's more, his bed wasn't slept in last night. He isn't in the library or the dining-room, and those three rooms are the only ones he ever uses. His habits, as you know, ma'am, are as regular as clockwork, as far as regards meals and so on. He takes his breakfast at nine o'clock, and goes from his breakfast to his library. He never left home in his life without letting me know beforehand. But he didn't sleep in this house last night, and he's not to be found in this house this morning.'

'He may have gone away last night with that strange gentleman,' suggested Bella.

'No, ma'am, that he didn't, for I let the foreign gentleman out, and locked the door after him.'

'Have you searched the house? Mr. Harefield may have fallen down in a fit somewhere. It's too dreadful to think of.'

'I've looked everywhere that was likely. There are only three rooms that he ever uses, as I said, ma'am. And I wouldn't frighten Miss Harefield for the world. That's why I came to consult you, ma'am, knowing you to be a clever young lady, and your father being my master's lawyer.'

'Come,' said Bella, seeing the two servants
looking at her, as if for inspiration. 'If Mr. Harefield has gone away on the spur of the moment,
I dare say he has left a letter or a memorandum
somewhere. Let us go round the house together,
and look about. It was quite right of you not to
disturb Miss Harefield.'

Bella led the way downstairs, followed by the
two scared servants. Her heart was beating fast,
agitated by nameless fears; but even in the midst
of her fear she felt a kind of elation, a sense of
new importance. Some great event was going to
happen. This slow old ship, the Water House,
was entering stormy seas, and she was at the
helm.

A sudden thought went through her heart like
a knife. What if Mr. Harefield were to die? His
death would mean wealth and freedom, love, liberty,
all glad things that earth could give for Beatrix.
It would mean union with Cyril Culverhouse.
The pang of envy which pierced Bella's little soul
at that thought was an almost insupportable agony.
She had endured the idea of their mutual love

with secret pangs and heart-burnings, but with at least an outward patience, while all possibility of their union was afar off. But, to see them prosperous lovers, happy in each other; to hear their wedding bells, and to have to sit by and smile assentingly while her little world praised them and rejoiced in their happiness, would be too much. All these considerations passed through her mind as she went downstairs, with the housekeeper and butler behind her, on her way to the library, where, if any letter had been left by Mr. Harefield before his departure, it was most likely to be found.

The shutters had been opened and the blinds drawn up, the fire was lighted, the chairs were set straight. But the large writing-table, with its litter of books and papers, had been left untouched. The housemaids at the Water House knew their duties too well to disturb anything there.

There were letters on the mantelpiece, old letters thrust carelessly behind bronze candlesticks and Oriental jars. The butler went over to

the hearth to examine these papers, with a faint
hope that there might be a message from his
missing master among them. The housekeeper
went to look at a tray in the hall, where cards
and letters were sometimes put, and where it was
just possible her master might have left some
message on a scrap of paper.

Bella turned over the books on the table—a
volume of Euripides, the last number of the *West-
minster*, half a dozen pamphlets, political and scien-
tific. She started, and looked at the butler, who
was standing with his back to her, deliberately
sorting the letters he had taken from the mantelpiece, chiefly receipted accounts which his master
had thrust there and forgotten, Christian Harefield
not being a man of business-like habits, or given
to the docketing and pigeon-holing of unimportant
papers.

Here, under Bella Scratchell's hand, lying half
hidden among the books and pamphlets, was a
letter that evidently meant something. A large
blue envelope, sealed with the Harefield crest, and
curiously addressed,—

'FOR MY DAUGHTER BEATRIX.'

A man would hardly write to his daughter, she living under the same roof with him, sitting at meat with him a few hours ago, unless he had something of an exceptional nature to tell her. These considerations and some more passed through Bella's mind as she stood with her hand on the letter, her eyes on the butler's portly back.

He was entirely engrossed with his scrutiny of the envelopes in his hand, being of a slow and stolid temperament, and requiring leisure in which to grasp an idea. At this moment no one but Bella and the writer knew of the existence of this letter.

And the writer, where was he?

Bella put the letter into her pocket.

"I will give it to her myself,' she thought. 'It will be better.'

'There's nothing here, Miss Scratchell,' said the butler, 'and this is where master always puts his letters for the post.'

And then he came and surveyed the table with his slow gaze, which seemed feebly to interrogate the covers of the books, as if in the hope that they might tell him something.

'Nothing on the table, ma'am ?'

'Nothing,' answered Bella.

'It's a very awkward position for old servants to find themselves placed in,' said the butler 'It isn't like my master to go out of the house and tell nobody, and leave his servants to puzzle and worry themselves about him. He has been eccentric of late years, but always the gentleman. And how could he go away, except on foot, which isn't likely ? I've been to the stables. He has not been out there. The horses are in their stalls. There's no coach goes through Little Yafford. There's no rail within five miles.'

'I wish 1 knew what to advise you,' said Bella, 'but indeed I do not. It's quite a dreadful situation for you to be in. And Miss Harefield will be coming downstairs presently, and must be told. I really think you ought to send for my father. He would know what to do, perhaps.'

'I couldn't take upon myself to do such a thing, ma'am. If my master should come back, and be offended at us making such a fuss——'

'But you have a right to make a fuss. His bed was not slept in last night, you say. He disappears suddenly on a Sunday night, after receiving a mysterious visitor. You have a right to be frightened.'

'Why frightened? Who has disappeared?' asked a voice at the door, and Beatrix entered, pallid and heavy eyed after her late slumbers.

'Oh, Beatrix,' cried Bella, going over to her, 'I did not think you were coming downstairs.'

'What is wrong?' asked Beatrix. 'Is it anything about my father?'

There was a pause, and then she turned sharply upon the butler.

'There is something wrong,' she said, 'and you are trying to hide it from me. Is my father ill?'

Peacock faltered, stammered, and finally explained the state of things.

'When did you last see papa?' asked Beatrix, after he had finished.

'It was half-past ten o'clock, ma'am. I brought wood and coals, and asked if there was anything more wanted, and my master said no.'

'Was he looking ill—or agitated?'

'I did not notice anything particular. He was sitting quietly before the fire.'

'Reading?'

'No. He was not reading.'

Beatrix sank into her father's chair, very pale, and trembling in every limb. She could think of nothing—she could suggest nothing. For the moment the very power of thought seemed suspended, but this state of mental collapse did not last long. Bella leant over her and murmured something indistinctly soothing. Beatrix rose and went quickly to the door.

'Let us look in every room in the house,' she said. 'In my mother's rooms first of all. He may be there.'

'Oh, Miss Beatrix!' cried Peacock, 'why, you know those rooms are never opened.'

'Yes, sometimes by him. He keeps the key.' The visitor last night was an old friend of my mother's. The sight of him might bring back thoughts of the past to my father.'

She ran quickly up stairs, and to the passage out of which her mother's rooms opened. It was at

the end of the house opposite that in which
Beatrix lived.

'See,' she cried, 'the key is in the door of the
morning-room. My father is there.'

She knocked softly, and waited for a minute or
so, but there was no answer. Then she took courage
and went in alone; while Peacock, and the housekeeper, and Miss Scratchell waited breathlessly in the
corridor.

There was a pause, which to these listeners
seemed long, and then there rose a cry that thrilled
them.

They went in all together, full of fear, and found
Beatrix Harefield on her knees beside a sofa, on
which, stretched at full length, clad in its monk's
robe of gray cloth, lay that which a few hours ago
had been the master of all things on the Water
House estate, ruler of many lives, by the sublime
right of ten thousand a year.

'Send some one for Mr. Namby,' cried Peacock.

'Come away with me, Miss Beatrix, love,' cried
the housekeeper. 'You can't do any good, and you'll

only make yourself unhappy. Come away with me and Miss Scratchell.'

Bella stood looking on, white and scared, and said not a word. Beatrix heard good Mrs. Peters' entreaties, but took no heed. She was still upon her knees, clasping a dead man's icy hand, and all the life within her seemed frozen like his.

CHAPTER II.

'DUST AND AN ENDLESS DARKNESS.'

THE church clock struck twelve, and, as the last stroke died into silence, Little Yafford school-house discharged a torrent of children into the rainy street, boys in red comforters, girls in blue comforters, comforters of the three primary colours and all their secondaries. Overcoats and cloaks were scarce at Little Yafford, and the worsted comforter was the chief winter clothing.

'Rain, rain, go away, come again another day,' shrieked the children, making a choral appeal to the clerk of the weather.

And they went whooping down the street, spinning tops, flying shuttlecocks, as if the rain were rather agreeable than otherwise.

Cyril Culverhouse came out of the school-house, unfurling his well-worn umbrella. He had been holding an examination of the scholars at the end of the year, and was disheartened at finding some of them woefully ignorant, despite the pains he had taken with both pupils and teachers during the last twelve months. It was uphill work. He found the children's minds fairly stored with a collection of hard facts. They knew all about the deluge, and the passage of the Red Sea. They could tell him the names of the prophets, and were as familiar with Daniel and Jonah as if the adventures of those holy men had been events of the last year; but of spiritual things, of the principles and meaning of their religion, they had hardly an idea. Here all was dark. They were Christians because they had been signed with the sign of the Cross, and sprinkled with holy water by the parson. Their catechisms told them all about that. But what Christianity meant, with its Divine law of love, justice, and mercy, they knew nothing.

Mr. Culverhouse sighed as he opened his umbrella and went out into the cold and rain. This Christmastide did not come upon him as a particularly happy season—save in its purely spiritual aspect. He was full of anxiety about Beatrix. It was hard to live so near her, and yet not dare to approach her. He had seen her in church every Sunday morning, and had seen her looking ill and worn. He knew that she was unhappy, and without a friend except Bella Scratchell. What a dismal season Christmas must seem for her, poor child! How cruel a mockery the joy-bells, and holly boughs, and outward semblance of festivity!

His business to-day took him the direction of the bridge. He could see the Water House on the other side of the river, its gray walls and ivy-covered entrance tower looming darkly through a mist of rain. Who was this approaching him along the muddy road, struggling manfully against wind and rain? Cyril could see nothing but a pair of pepper and salt legs under a gingham umbrella. The pepper and salt legs brought the umbrella nearer him. It was an umbrella with a slippery brass handle, and altogether an affliction to its possessor. A sudden gust blew it on one side, and revealed the countenance of Mr. Namby, pale and agitated.

'How d'ye do, Namby?' said Cyril, with no

intention of saying more, for the village surgeon was a talkative little man, and the busy curate had no time to waste upon gossip. But Mr. Namby made a dead stop.

'Oh, Mr. Culverhouse, I have just come from the Water House.' This was enough to bring Cyril to a standstill also. 'There is awful trouble there.'

'Good heavens! What trouble? Is Miss Harefield ill?'

'Poor child! She is in a dreadful state. Her father is dead.'

Cyril felt as if his heart had stopped beating. The rainy landscape rocked before his eyes, the muddy road reeled beneath his feet.

'Dead!' he gasped.

'Dead, suddenly. And I'm afraid by poison.'

'What!' cried Cyril. 'You must be mad to say such a thing.'

'It will be for the coroner to decide; there will be an inquest, of course. But I have no doubt as to the cause of death. There are all the symptoms of poisoning by opium.'

'Good God! Was he in the habit of taking opium?'

'Not to my knowledge.'

'But he surely must have been. How else should he come by his death? It must have been an over dose of opium.'

'I never heard him complain of acute pain. He had an iron constitution. He had no reason for taking opium that I can see.'

'No reason! Look at the men who take it without reason, for the pleasure of taking it. Look at Coleridge—De Quincey. Mr. Harefield was just the kind of man to be an opium-eater. That would account for his hermit-like life existence—his seclusion from all the world. He had a world of his own—he had the opium-eater's paradise.'

'It is possible,' said Mr. Namby, doubtfully. 'But it is strange that I should never have perceived the symptoms. There are unmistakable indications in the appearance of the habitual opium-eater.'

'How often did you see Mr. Harefield?'

'Not very often, I confess.'

'Not often enough for your observations of him to be worth much. Dead! It is very awful. When did it happen?'

Mr. Namby proceeded to relate all he had heard at the Water House; and for once in his life he found Cyril Culverhouse a patient listener.

'And Miss Harefield? How does she bear the shock?'

'She is very quiet. She seems stupefied. The whole thing was so sudden. She and Miss Scratchell dined with Mr. Harefield yesterday evening. There was nothing to show that he was ill or agitated, or in any way different from his usual self.'

'Who is with Miss Harefield?'

'Only Miss Scratchell and the servants. That excellent Miss Scales is away in Devonshire, with an ailing relation; but she is expected back daily.'

'She ought to be summoned at once. I'll call at the Vicarage and ask Mrs. Dulcimer to go to the Water House.'

He turned back with Mr. Namby, and they walked together towards the Vicarage, which was at the other end of the village street.

Mr. Namby turned into his own garden gate, and left Cyril to go on alone to the Vicarage. Mr. Culverhouse had no exalted opinion of Mrs. Dulcimer's good sense, but he highly estimated her good nature, and he could think of no one better whose friendship he could appeal to on Beatrix Harefield's behalf. Mrs. Dulcimer was warmly attached to Beatrix. She would be overflowing with kindliness and sympathy in this hour of trouble.

The Vicar was in his library, Mrs. Dulcimer in the dining-room with Rebecca, allotting little heaps of warm clothing as Christmas gifts for her poor parishioners. The dining-table was covered with neatly made flannels and linsey petticoats. Mrs. Dulcimer and Rebecca were folding and smoothing the little packages, and admiring their own work, for Rebecca's needle was as busy as her mistress's in this benevolent labour.

Rebecca withdrew respectfully, at the curate's

entrance, and Cyril told Mrs. Dulcimer what had happened at the Water House. She interrupted him continually with questions and exclamations; but he got through his story somehow.

'Poor dear child!' cried Mrs. Dulcimer, when she had heard all; 'coming into that fine estate; poor Mr. Harefield's mother was a Pynsent, you know, and all the Pynsent property goes with the Harefield estate, and under such shocking circumstances. What a pity she hasn't a husband to protect her interests! I shouldn't wonder if the property were thrown into Chancery. If your cousin Kenrick had only been wise now——'

'What do you mean, Mrs. Dulcimer?'

'He might have been owner of the finest property in the West Riding. He might have been Beatrix's husband by this time.'

'I think the lady would have been entitled to a voice in the matter,' said Cyril, 'however wise my cousin Kenrick might have been.'

'Oh, nonsense, Cyril! Such a young man as Kenrick might choose for himself. And in poor Beatrix's position she would naturally have re-

ciprocated his affection, if it had only been
warmly offered.'

'I cannot agree with you there. But if you
will go and see the poor girl——'

'I'll put on my bonnet this instant. Will you
come with me, Cyril?'

'I think not, I should be of no use.'

'Well, a man certainly is apt to be in the
way under such circumstances. He never knows
what to say, or what to leave unsaid.'

'And a woman never errs in leaving anything
unsaid,' remarked the Vicar, entering through the
curtained archway.

While Mrs. Dulcimer was putting on her
bonnet, Cyril told the Vicar what Mr. Namby
had said about the cause of Christian Harefield's
death, a detail which he had not communicated
to Mrs. Dulcimer.

'This makes it a painful business,' said Cyril.

'Very,' answered the Vicar. 'But I should not
be surprised at Mr. Harefield having deliberately
taken the dose that killed him.'

'Why not?'

'Because to my mind he was a likely subject for suicide. Look at the life he led. A man must sooner or later get tired of leading such a life. Some day he must say to himself, "Wherefore, to what end do I live?" And then, if he is half an infidel, if religion exercises no restraining influence over his acts, he will make up his mind, suddenly, perhaps, to end his existence. He has no love of his fellow-men to anchor him to earth, no hope of anything bright or good waiting for him in the coming years. He has a very faint belief—possibly none at all—in a tribunal beyond this world where he will have to answer for his deeds. It is very clear to me that for the last ten years Christian Harefield's life has been burdened by some incurable sorrow. He may have grown weary of bearing the sorrow, as people grow weary of bearing pain.'

'You are probably right,' said Cyril; 'yet I should rather believe his death accidental.'

Mrs. Dulcimer went to the Water House, knowing no more than the fact of Mr. Harefield's sudden death and his daughter's desolation. She went up to Beatrix's room, expecting that the stricken girl would throw herself into her arms and pour out all her woes upon that friendly bosom. Mrs. Dulcimer's frills and puffings and broad bonnet-strings were in a flutter with the importance of her mission. She felt as if she were the young heiress's legal guardian.

'My dearest girl,' she cried, 'how my heart bleeds for you!'

But Beatrix was in a curious mood. She seemed not to want other people's bleeding hearts. Indeed, her own heart was too deeply wounded to receive comfort from such sympathetic bleeding.

Mrs. Dulcimer made all the customary speeches which are made and provided for such occasions.

'You must come to the Vicarage with me, my love,' she said. 'You must not stop in this dreary house.'

But here Beatrix was firm. She would not leave the house in which her dead father was lying.

'We were not happy together while he was living,' she said, 'but I will not desert him now he is dead.'

And then she relapsed into a state of seeming apathy, from which Mrs. Dulcimer found it impossible to rouse her. Bella was there, looking pale and scared, but ready to be useful if she were required.

By and by, failing in all attempts at consolation, Mrs. Dulcimer went downstairs to talk this sad business over with the housekeeper and Mr. Scratchell, who had appeared upon the scene as legal representative of the deceased, and had already busied himself in a semi-official manner in locking up papers and setting seals on desks and cabinets in the library.

From the butler and housekeeper Mrs. Dulcimer heard details which she had not heard from Cyril Culverhouse. She was told all about the mysterious visitor of the previous night.

'I believe he was one of Mrs. Harefield's Italian friends,' said the butler. 'There was something familiar about his face. I could as good as swear I've seen him times and often before last night.'

'As good as swearing won't do,' said Mr.

Scratchell, with professional severity. 'Unless you are prepared to make a direct statement upon oath you had better say nothing, about your impressions and recollections before the coroner by and by.'

'The coroner!' cried Mrs. Dulcimer, with a look of horror. 'What has the coroner to do with it?'

'Why, my dear madam, as Mr. Harefield's death is both sudden and mysterious, there will naturally be an inquest. The notices have been sent round to the jury already, I believe, and the inquiry will be held here this afternoon. To-morrow being Christmas Day, you see, allows of no time being lost.'

'Oh, this is too dreadful!' exclaimed Mrs. Dulcimer; 'that poor girl, without a single relation, in a house of death, under such fearful circumstances. I must get her away.'

'I would strongly recommend you to do nothing of the kind. Miss Harefield had better stop here. She will be wanted as a witness, for it was she who discovered her father's death. Her leaving the house might create a scandal. She need not be alone. Bella can stay with her.'

'Poor girl,' sighed Mrs. Dulcimer 'What a position!'

And then, the ruling passion still dominant in her mind, she thought of Sir Kenrick Culverhouse, and what an opportunity this time of trouble might afford for the ripening of friendship into love. It was a time in which a young woman would naturally lean upon a masculine mind for support and guidance, in which words of comfort would sound stronger from masculine lips.

'If Kenrick were only here to-day,' thought Mrs. Dulcimer.

And then she remembered that Sir Kenrick had given her a half-promise that he would come back to Yorkshire in time to eat his Christmas dinner at the Vicarage.

CHAPTER III.

BEFORE THE CORONER.

AT the table where Christian Harefield had sat at
meat on Sunday evening, with his daughter and his
daughter's companion, sat the coroner, in the gather-
ing dusk of Monday afternoon, with his jurymen in
a row of heavy oaken chairs on either side of him—
looking very much as if they were sitting at a new
Barmecide's dinner—to inquire into the cause or
causes of Christian Harefield's death.

The inquest had been called for three o'clock,
but it was nearly four, and the proceedings were
but just beginning. There had been the usual
delays—one or two jurymen late—a good deal of
blundering in calling over the names—some small
disputations about nothing particular—a general
muddling away of time. And now the sky outside
the heavy mullioned casements was deepening from
gray to dun, the red glow of the fire was shining

redder upon the oak panelling as the outside world
darkened, the ticking of the clock on the chimney-
piece sounded obtrusively above the half-whispered
conversation, and the falling of a cinder on the
hearth seemed as startling as the report of a gun.

Mr. Scratchell sat at a corner of the table,
note-book in hand, to watch the proceedings as
Miss Harefield's legal adviser. He had appointed
himself to that post, and no one had disputed his
right to it. Beatrix had asked for no legal advice.
She knew that her father was dead, suddenly, mysteriously, awfully, but no instinct of her mind impelled her to seek comfort, counsel, or succour from
Mr. Scratchell, or to throw herself into the sanctuary
of English law.

The coroner was Dr. Judson, of Great Yafford,
a medical man much respected in his district, and
a coroner who indulged in the eccentricity of thinking for himself.

The proceedings were opened by the examination
of Mr. Namby, who gave his opinion very decidedly
upon the cause of death. He had no doubt upon
this point. The deceased gentleman had died from

an overdose of opium. He described those indications which led him to believe this, and Dr. Judson, who knew Taylor's Medical Jurisprudence by heart, knew that the witness was right.

Peacock, the butler, the last person who had seen Mr. Harefield alive, was the first witness examined, after the medical evidence had been heard, and the jury had withdrawn to view the body.

He described the visit of the foreign gentleman, and his departure. He was not able to recall the gentleman's name, although he had glanced at his card before he carried it to Mr. Harefield. The name was a foreign one, and had slipped out of his memory directly after he read it.

Coroner. How long was he with your master?

Peacock. It might be from an hour to an hour and a half. We were just beginning our suppers in the servants' hall when the bell rang, and I opened the door to the strange gentleman. We hadn't finished many minutes when Mr. Harefield rung his bell for me to let the strange gentleman out.

Coroner. Do you usually take an hour and a half at your supper ?

Peacock. We might take as much on a Sunday night.

Coroner (with grim facetiousness, reflecting that this is how his servants make such an impression on the butcher's bill). Oh, I see, on Sunday night you eat a little extra. The better the day the better the deed. Then, as you are in the habit of sitting an hour and a half at your supper, you conclude that the stranger was with Mr. Harefield as long as that.

Peacock. I should say about that time.

Coroner. How often did you see Mr. Harefield after the stranger left ?

Peacock. I went into the room twice— once with some fresh logs, once with coals.

Coroner. Did you observe anything peculiar in your master's manner ?

Peacock. No, sir. When I went in the first time he was sitting before the fire, a little moody-like, staring straight before him ; but he was moody in his ways most times. When I went in with the coals, he was sitting there still—like a statue. I asked

him if there was anything more wanted, and he said,
'No, Peacock, nothing more.' That was his general
reply. I couldn't see any difference in his voice or
manner.

Coroner. Were you with Miss Harefield this
morning when she discovered her father's death?

Peacock. I was just outside the door when she
went in and found him lying dead upon the sofa.

Coroner. In which room was he found?

Peacock. In Mrs. Harefield's sitting-room. It
hadn't entered into my head—or into the housekeeper's
head—to look for him in that room, for the room was
never used. Mr. Harefield kept the key, and it was
kept locked at all times, like a tomb.

Coroner. Who suggested looking into that room?

Peacock. Miss Harefield. 'Let us go into every
room in the house,' she said, 'my mother's rooms
first of all.'

Coroner. Did she give any reason for making
that suggestion?

Peacock. Yes—she named her reason. The
strange gentleman was an old friend of her mother's,
Miss Harefield thought, and that might have set her

father thinking of old times, and carried his thoughts back to his wife's rooms. That is what I understood her to mean.

Coroner. Then Miss Harefield led the way to the room in which her father was found ?

Peacock. She did.

Coroner. And he was quite dead when you found him ?

Peacock. Quite dead. When Mr. Namby saw my master he said he must have been dead some hours. He was stone cold—icy cold. Mr. Namby said icy coldness of the body was one of the signs of poisoning by opium.

Coroner. You need not tell us what Mr. Namby said. Mr. Namby has told us his opinion. Have you any knowledge of your master taking opium, for any purpose whatever ?

Peacock. I have never known him to do such a thing.

Coroner. What ! not an occasional dose to deaden pain ?

Peacock. I have never heard him complain of pain.

Coroner. But have you never had cause to suspect him of taking opium? He was a man of reserved and lonely habits. Have you never seen him in a stupefied, dreamy state, such as you may have heard of or read of as peculiar to opium eaters?

Peacock. Never.

Coroner. Have you ever seen any bottle containing opium, or any bottle labelled opium, or laudanum, in his rooms?

Peacock. Never.

Coroner. Have you ever seen anything in your late master's manner indicating a disturbed state of mind—the sort of thing which is usually called not being quite right in one's mind?

Peacock. No, sir. My late master was not a cheerful man. He was a gentleman who preferred to live alone. He had always lived shut up in his own rooms since his wife's death. I believe he took her death very much to heart. He has never talked about his troubles to me, or to any one in the house, but I believe that was his trouble.

The next witness was Isabella Scratchell. She

had been present at the discovery of Mr. Harefield's death. She had dined with him on the previous evening, and would naturally be an independent witness, and a more unbiassed judge of his demeanour and mental condition than either his old servants or his daughter.

Bella gave her evidence with a graceful timidity and a gentle firmness which charmed her hearers. She felt that it was her first public appearance, and that the eyes of Little Yafford—or possibly of a much wider world than Little Yafford—were upon her. She stood at the end of the long table, with her clear blue eyes fixed respectfully upon the coroner, her little white hands clasped, her head slightly bent. Even her father's cold eye perceived that there was grace and prettiness in this familiar face and figure.

'A girl like that ought to get a husband able to support her,' thought Mr. Scratchell, who regarded marriage as an institution devised for taking daughters off a father's hands, and throwing the onus of maintaining them upon an obliging stranger.

Coroner. You dined with Mr. Harefield yesterday evening, I believe?

Bella. Yes.

Coroner. What impression did his manner make upon you?

Bella. I felt very sorry for Beatrix—for Miss Harefield.

Coroner. Why?

Bella. It was so sad to see a father and daughter so unloving. Or I should say sad to see a daughter so little loved.

Coroner. Then you conclude the want of affection was on Mr. Harefield's side?

Bella (after a moment of hesitation). Yes.

Coroner. Do you mean that Mr. Harefield was absolutely harsh in his treatment of his daughter?

Bella. Both harsh and cold. I should have felt it painfully had I been Miss Harefield. Indeed, I know she did feel it.

Coroner. She has told you so?

Bella. Indirectly. She has told me of unhappiness between her and her father.

Coroner. What kind of unhappiness?

Bella. I had rather not enter into that. I have no right to betray Miss Harefield's confidence.

Coroner. You are bound to answer any questions bearing upon the subject of this inquiry. I want particularly to know the state of feeling between Mr. Harefield and his daughter. Now what was the unhappiness of which you have spoken?

Bella (with her eyes wandering piteously round the stolid faces of the jury, and at last seeking counsel in the looks of her father). Am I really obliged to answer this question?

Scratchell. Yes, yes, girl, you'd better answer.

Bella. The unhappiness was about a gentleman to whom Miss Harefield is deeply attached. Mr. Harefield forbade her to see this gentleman, or to hold any communication with him.

Coroner. And that had been the cause of ill-feeling between the father and daughter?

Bella. I have never said ill-feeling. I only say that Mr. Harefield's manner to his daughter was morose and unkind.

Coroner. Did you perceive anything approaching to eccentricity or mental disturbance in his manner last evening?

Bella. Nothing.

Coroner. Should you consider him a man likely to commit suicide?

Bella. I should say not. He was always reserved and gloomy.

Coroner. But not more so yesterday evening than usual?

Bella. No more than usual.

Coroner. How did Miss Harefield seem impressed by the discovery of her father's death?

Bella. She seemed stunned.

Coroner. She said very little, I conclude?

Bella. She said nothing. The awfulness of the discovery seemed to turn her to stone.

The next and last witness was one in whom even those stolid jurymen felt a keen interest. The next witness was Beatrix Harefield, who came into the room slowly, leaning upon Mrs. Dulcimer, a living image of horror and amazement.

Some one, seeing how feebly she moved from

the door to the table, brought her a chair; or, in the richer phraseology of the reporters, she was 'accommodated with a seat.' She sat, looking straight at the distant coroner, seen dimly by the light of tall wax candles in old silver candelabra, at the end of an avenue of jurymen.

Beatrix was questioned as to the finding of her father's body. Her replies were at first hardly audible, but voice and manner grew firmer as she went on.

Coroner. What induced you to suggest that your mother's sitting-room should be the first place to be searched?

Beatrix. Because I fancied my father's thoughts would dwell upon my mother last night.

Coroner. Why?

Beatrix. The gentleman who came here—after an absence of many years—was a countryman and friend of my mother's. That would carry my father's thoughts back.

Coroner. Can you tell me the name of this gentleman? His evidence would be important as to the state of your father's mind yesterday evening.

Beatrix. I have heard him called Antonio.

Coroner. That was his Christian name, no doubt. Have you never heard his surname ?

Beatrix. Never, to my knowledge. I was a child when he used to visit here. I have heard my father and mother both speak of him as Antonio.

Coroner. Was your father in the habit of going into that locked up room of your mother's ?

Beatrix. I know he went there sometimes.

Coroner. How do you know that ?

Beatrix. I found the key left in the door once. No one could have left it there but my father.

Coroner. The room was kept locked, I understand. The members of the household were not allowed to go in.

Beatrix. It was kept locked from every one for ten years.

Coroner. Have you never been in the room during that time ?

Beatrix. Once only. The day I found the key in the door. I went in and looked at my mother's room.

Coroner. Have you any reason to suppose that your father was in the habit of taking opium?

Beatrix. I have no reason to suppose so. We lived very much apart, but from what I saw of his mode of life, I do not think my father ever took opium.

Coroner. You have never heard him complain of pain of any kind—rheumatism or neuralgia, for instance—which might have induced him to seek relief from opiates?

Beatrix. Never.

Coroner. Do you know whether there was any laudanum in the house at the time of your father's death?

Beatrix (with evident agitation, and after a noticeable pause). No, there was no laudanum in the house at the time of my father's death.

Coroner. Are you sure of that?

Beatrix. Quite sure. I have suffered from sleeplessness for many weeks. Last week I bought a little laudanum, and have been taking it nightly in small doses. I took rather a larger dose than usual last night and emptied the bottle.

The jury, who had been getting a little absent-minded during what they considered a somewhat wire-drawn interrogation, became suddenly on the alert. Four and twenty eyes were fixed inquisitively upon the pale face of the witness. A gentleman who stood in the shadow of the doorway watching the proceedings grew a shade paler than he had been before.

Coroner. Did any one know of your taking this laudanum?

Beatrix. No one.

Coroner. Was it recommended by your medical adviser?

Beatrix. No. I asked Mr. Namby to give me opiates, but he refused.

Coroner. And, unknown to every one, you bought laudanum, and took it in nightly doses?

Beatrix. Yes. The sleepless nights were so miserable. I think I should have gone mad if they had continued much longer.

Coroner. Was there any cause for these sleepless nights?

Beatrix (faltering, and with a distressed look). I had been unhappy lately.

Coroner. There was a love affair, was there not, which your father disapproved?

Beatrix. Yes.

Coroner. Was there ill-feeling between you and your father about this love affair?

Beatrix. Not exactly ill-feeling. I thought that my father acted unkindly.

Coroner. There was no quarrel between you?

Beatrix. No. I submitted to my father's will, but he knew that when I came of age I should fulfil the engagement of which he disapproved.

Coroner. In other words, you defied him?

Beatrix. No. I only told him that I should be faithful to the man I loved.

Coroner. No matter how objectionable that person might be to your father?

Beatrix. He had no cause to object. He ought to have been proud that I had won the love of so good a man.

Coroner. Perhaps a young lady is not always the best judge upon that point. Now, will you tell me where you got this laudanum?

Beatrix. At Great Yafford.

Coroner. At which chemist's ?

Beatrix. I got it from several chemists. The chemist I first went to would give me only a very small quantity. I went on to another chemist and got a little more.

Coroner. That was very ingenious. How many chemists did you go to in this manner ?

Beatrix. I believe I went to five or six shops.

Coroner. Getting a little laudanum at each. How much did you get altogether ?

Beatrix. When I emptied all the bottles into one there was a small bottle full.

Coroner. I should like to see the bottle. Let it be sent for.

Beatrix. It is in the little Indian cabinet on the writing-table in my bedroom.

The bottle was fetched at the coroner's desire. It was an ounce bottle, quite empty, labelled in the usual manner.

Coroner. Was this bottle never out of your hands after you brought it home.?

Beatrix. Never. Till last night I kept it locked in my dressing-case.

Coroner.   You are sure of that ?

Beatrix.   I am quite sure.

This ended Beatrix Harefield's examination. After this the coroner adjourned the inquiry for a week, with a view to obtaining further evidence. He made a strong point of the desirability of obtaining the evidence of the strange visitor who had been closeted with Mr. Harefield for an hour and a half on the night before his death.

CHAPTER IV.

CHRISTMAS EVE.

BEATRIX went back to her room, accompanied by
Mrs. Dulcimer and Bella Scratchell. In going
through the dimly-lighted hall she passed a group of
figures standing close together near the foot of the
staircase; the Vicar, Mr. Namby, and one other, a
taller figure than either of the two, a man standing
with half-averted face, listening to some remark of
Mr. Dulcimer's. Towards this one, whose face was
hidden, Beatrix looked intently, but there was no
time for more than that one earnest look, for Mrs.
Dulcimer's supporting arm was round her, and Bella
was on the other side. Between these sympathisers,
she was led up the shallow old stairs to the familiar
corridor which had to-night so awful and even unknown an air. Death lay yonder in the bedchamber
where the coroner and his jury had gone in silently

half an hour ago, to look upon the marble form that had so lately been master and owner of all things at the Water House. In the place of that stern ruler there was now only the lifeless clay. A dreadful blankness and emptiness had descended upon the house, so quiet, so changeless heretofore, but now pervaded with the one idea of death.

Beatrix shivered as she passed the door of the room where her dead father was lying. Mrs. Dulcimer perceived that shuddering recoil, and again suggested that her sweet Beatrix should come to the Vicarage. But again Beatrix was firm.

'Do you think I am frightened at the thought of death?' she asked bitterly. 'My father's life was a living death—to me. He is no further removed from me now than he was yesterday.'

'My dear child, if I could stay with you here, I would not so much mind,' said Mrs. Dulcimer, 'but I shall be obliged to go back to the Vicarage almost immediately. There is Clement's tea. He would not think of sitting down to tea without me if he were ever so hungry. And then later in the evening there will be the carol singers. We always give them cake and hot elder wine. So you see, my love, I shall be obliged to go.'

Beatrix gave a weary sigh.

'Indeed, dear Mrs. Dulcimer, I shall be better alone,' she said. 'I am grateful for your kindness, but I would rather be alone. I do not want even Bella, and I am sure it is cruel to keep her in this melancholy house. Do go home, Bella, or go to the Vicarage with Mrs. Dulcimer and hear the carols.'

'Beatrix, how can you suppose that I would leave you?' exclaimed Bella, and again Beatrix sighed wearily.

It would have been an infinite relief to her to be quite alone. She had recognised Cyril in that little group in the hall, and he had let her pass, without one word of consolation, without one pitying look. He must have known that she was passing, she told herself, and he had kept his face averted; he had stood coldly by and made no sign of sympathy or kindly feeling.

Mrs. Dulcimer tied her bonnet strings, kissed Beatrix repeatedly, promised to come and see her directly after morning service next day, and then hurried off to superintend the Vicar's evening meal.

'I shouldn't be surprised if Kenrick was to pop in upon us to-night,' she said, as she was going away. 'He promised to spend Christmas with us.'

Beatrix gave a little start at Kenrick's name. He was so near Cyril in her mind, and just now she was deeply moved by Cyril's strange coldness.

Mrs. Dulcimer saw her startled look, and had an inward movement of triumph. Here was one of her good-natured schemes assuredly about to prosper. Kenrick had evidently made an impression upon Beatrix; and now death had made Beatrix mistress of a splendid fortune.

'I only hope that foolish boy will remember his engagement to eat his Christmas dinner with us,' thought the Vicar's wife, as she trudged sturdily homewards, with her petticoats held well out of the mud, and her country-made boots defying the slushy road.

When Mrs. Dulcimer had gone the two girls sat at opposite sides of the hearth, very much as they had been seated the night before, only there was no pretence of reading to-night. Beatrix sat looking idly at the fire with great melancholy eyes. Bella watched her, ready to offer any scrap of consolation which might suggest itself.

'It seems painfully clear that my father committed suicide,' Beatrix said, at the end of a long reverie.

'Oh, I hope not,' exclaimed Bella, piously. 'We must not think that, dear. He may have taken an overdose of laudanum.'

'Yes, if he had been in the habit of taking laudanum. But he was not.'

'How can you know that? Poor Mr. Harefield was so reserved. He lived so much apart from you.'

'But if he had taken laudanum habitually somebody would have known of it. Peacock, for instance, who always waited upon him. No, Bella, there was something in that Italian's visit. I believe my father poisoned himself.'

'But why?'

'For the last ten years his life has been one long regret. Yes. I am sure of that now. His coldness and unkindness to me were the growth of despair.

He told me that he had closed his heart against all human affection ten years ago. That was the time of my mother's death. And last night those long years of grief culminated in a paroxysm of despair, and in a rash moment—a moment in which he was not responsible for his actions—he threw away his life.'

'But how did he come by the poison?' asked Bella. 'He must have obtained the poison somehow. That would be a deliberate act—just as deliberate as yours when you went into six different chemists' shops.'

"Why do you look at me like that, Bella?' inquired Beatrix, struck by something curious in the other's intent gaze. 'Do you suppose that I did not tell the truth about the laudanum I bought at Great Yafford?'

'I know you told the truth. I was with you in the pony carriage, you know. Don't you remember my asking the meaning of all those little packages? I was only thinking, just now, that had I been you I don't think I should have told the coroner about that laudanum.'

'Why not? There was no harm in my buying it. I had as much right to buy that as any other medicine.'

'Of course, dear. But still I am sorry you told about it.'

'Why, in goodness name?'

'Because it might make a bad impression upon some people—people who don't know you as your friends know you. People who think that you and your father lived unhappily together. It might put curious ideas into their heads.'

'Bella, what do you mean?' cried Beatrix, starting up from her chair. 'Do you mean that there is any creature on this earth so vile in mind and heart as to be capable of believing that I poisoned my father?'

'My dear Beatrix, there are people wicked enough to be ready to believe anything evil of those who are richer than themselves.'

'I am sorry such a hideous suggestion should come from you, Bella,' said Beatrix, coldly.

Bella saw that she had gone a little too far, and knelt down by her dear Beatrix's chair, and tried to soothe the irritation her suggestions had caused. Beatrix's wounded feeling was not easily appeased.

'If such a thing can enter into the mind of my earliest friend, my old playfellow, what measure of evil am I to expect from strangers?' she said.

'My dearest Beatrix, have I been speaking of my own thoughts? I only said I was sorry you mentioned those unfortunate purchases at Yafford.'

'I shall never be sorry for having spoken the truth.'

Mrs. Dulcimer had her wish gratified. At the gate of the Vicarage a large and blundering vehicle loomed upon her through the rainy darkness. It was one of the Great Yafford flies, a cumbrous conveyance of wood, iron, and mouldy leather, which Mr. Bollen, of 'The George,' innkeeper and postmaster, facetiously called a landau.

'Have you brought any one from the town?' asked Mrs. Dulcimer.

'Yes, mum, I've bringed a gen'leman from t' steation.'

Mrs. Dulcimer went into the house delighted. She forgot the awfulness of things at the Water House, forgot everything but this propitious arrival of Sir Kenrick.

'My dear Kenrick!' she exclaimed, making a friendly rush at the newly-arrived guest, as he stood in the hall talking to the Vicar. 'How good of you to remember your promise!'

'My dear Mrs. Dulcimer, do you suppose there is any house in which I would sooner spend my Christmas than in this? But what terrible news this is about Mr. Harefield.'

'Is it not awful? Poor Beatrix, without a relative; and with hardly a friend except Clement and myself. With her great wealth, too—for now she is mistress of everything.'

'There is no one else, I suppose, to whom Mr. Harefield can have left his estates?'

'Not a creature. He lived like a hermit, and Beatrix is his only child. It is a great fortune for a girl to be mistress of.'

'Is it really so large a fortune?' inquired Kenrick, in a conversational tone, taking off his coat and wraps.

'Immense. Mr. Harefield's mother was old Mr. Pynsent's only daughter, and a great heiress. There is the Lincolnshire property. I have heard Mr. Scratchell say that it brings in more than the Yorkshire estate.'

'In plain words, Beatrix will have something like ten thousand a year,' said the Vicar, rather impatiently. 'A great deal too much money for any young woman, and likely to be a burden instead of a blessing.'

'Not if she marries an honourable man, Clement,' remonstrated Mrs. Dulcimer. 'All depends upon how she marries. She ought to marry some one who can give her position. She does not want a rich husband.'

Mr. Dulcimer sighed.

'If our English Church had what it ought to have, educational establishments for women, I should recommend Beatrix to avoid the rocks and shoals of matrimony, and bestow her wealth upon

such an institution. She could live very happily
as the foundress and superior of a Protestant convent, like Madame de Maintenon, at St. Cyr.'

'With this difference,' said Sir Kenrick.
'Madame de Maintenon was an old woman, and
had had two husbands.'

'But her only period of happiness was at St. Cyr.'

'So she said ; yet she intrigued considerably
to be Queen of France, *à la main gauche.*'

'Clement!' exclaimed Mrs. Dulcimer, looking
the image of horror ; 'the word convent makes
me shudder. When a Protestant clergyman talks
approvingly of convents, people may well say we
are drifting towards Rome.'

'Please, 'um, the fowls are getting as cold as
ice,' said Rebecca, at the door of the dining-room.
'Do let me take your bonnet and shawl, 'um.'

They all went in, Mrs. Dulcimer having removed her wraps, and shaken out her frillings
hastily. The dining-table looked the picture of
comfort, with its composite meal, half tea, half
supper, a pair of fowls roasted to what Rebecca
called 'a turn,' a dish of broiled ham, a cold sir-

loin and a winter salad, made as only Rebecca—
taught by the Vicar himself—could make salads.
Kenrick had a fine appetite after his long damp
journey from the South.'

All tea-time the talk was of Mr. Harefield and
Beatrix. The Vicar had been in the little group of
listeners standing by the door of the Water House
dining-room, and had heard the whole of the coroner's
inquiry.

'That poor girl ought to have somebody to watch
the proceedings on her behalf,' said Mr. Dulcimer. 'I
shall go over to Great Yafford on Wednesday and see
Mivers. He is about the cleverest lawyer in the town.'

'Mr. Scratchell would surely protect Beatrix's
interests,' suggested Mrs. Dulcimer.

'Mr. Scratchell is very good as a collector of
rents, but I do not give him credit for being exactly
the man for a critical position.'

'What do you mean by a critical position,
Clement?' exclaimed Mrs. Dulcimer.

'I mean that Beatrix's position is a very critical
one. Her admission that she bought laudanum at
six different shops, within one week of her father's

death by that poison, is calculated to raise very painful suspicions in the minds of those who do not know the girl's nature as well as you and I do.'

'Oh, Clement, how dreadful!'

'To protect her against such suspicion she must have a clever lawyer. Mr. Harefield must have got the laudanum that killed him somewhere or other. The mode and manner of his getting it ought to be found out before this day week.'

'It must be found out!' exclaimed Mrs. Dulcimer. 'Kenrick, you will help this poor ill-used girl, will you not? Your chivalry will be aroused in her defence.'

'I am sure if I can be of any use'—faltered Kenrick.

'You can't,' said the Vicar. 'A clever lawyer will be of use—and no one else. I shall write to Mivers directly after tea.'

'Has Miss Harefield any idea that the admission she made about the laudanum may be dangerous?' inquired Kenrick.

'Not the slightest. Poor girl, she is simply dazed—that is the word—dazed! She did not even

want me to stay with her. She did not care whether
I stayed or went away. Her brain is in a state of
stupor.'

'It was very lucky for her that she did make
that statement about her purchase of the laudanum,'
said the Vicar.

'But why, if the admission was likely to do her
harm?' asked Kenrick.

'Because to have concealed the fact would have
done her more harm. The chemists from whom she
bought the stuff would have talked about it.'

'Of course,' assented Mrs. Dulcimer, 'everything
is talked about in Great Yafford. Though it is such a
large town, it is almost as bad as a village for gossip.'

Not at the Vicarage only, but at every tea table in
Little Yafford the inquest at the Water House was
the only subject of conversation. Though very few
people, save those actually concerned, had crossed the
threshold of the house during the inquiry, yet everybody seemed to know all about it. They knew what
the butler had said, what Mr. Namby had said, what
Beatrix and Bella had said—how each and every

witness had looked—and the different degrees of
emotion with which each particular witness had
given his or her evidence. Opinions at present were
distinguished by their vagueness. There was a
general idea that Mr. Harefield's death was a very
mysterious affair—that a great deal more would come
out at the next inquiry—that the butler and Bella
Scratchell were both keeping back a great deal—that
Beatrix and her father had lived much more unhappily
together than anybody had hitherto suspected—that
Beatrix, being of Italian origin on the mother's side,
was likely to do strange things. In support of which
sweeping conclusion the better informed gossips cited
the examples of Lucretia Borgia, Beatrice Cenci, and
a young woman christened Bianca, whose surname
nobody was able to remember.

Late in the evening Cyril Culverhouse came to
the Vicarage. He had promised to be there to hear
the carol singers, in whom, as his own scholars, he
was bound to be interested. He was looking pale
and worried, and Mrs. Dulcimer immediately
suggested a tumbler of Rebecca's port wine negus,'
a restorative which the curate obstinately refused.

'I am a little anxious about your friend Miss Harefield,' he said. 'I have written to a London lawyer to come down here immediately and protect her interests.'

'And I have written to Mr. Mivers, of Great Yafford,' said the Vicar. 'She ought to be well looked after between us.'

'You were with her after the inquest, Mrs. Dulcimer,' said Cyril, 'How did she seem?'

'Dazed,' exclaimed Mrs. Dulcimer, exactly as she had exclaimed before. 'There is no other word for it. She reminded me of a sleep-walker.'

CHAPTER V.

GLOOMY DAYS.

MRS. DULCIMER called at the Water House after the morning service on Christmas Day. She found Beatrix alone, and very quiet, disinclined to talk of her grief, or, indeed, to talk about any subject whatever. Bella had gone to assist at the early dinner at the Park, or, in other words, to see that the juvenile Pipers did not gorge themselves with turkey and pudding.

'You ought not to have let Bella leave you, my love,' said Mrs. Dulcimer. 'It is dreadful for you to be alone.'

'Dear Mrs. Dulcimer, Bella cannot do me any good. She cannot bring my father back to life, or explain the mystery of his death. I insisted upon her going to the Park to-day. I am really better alone.'

'My poor Beatrix, I cannot understand you.'

'Am I so eccentric in liking to sit by my fireside quietly, and suffer in silence?' asked Beatrix, with a wintry smile. 'I should have thought any one would have preferred that to being the object of perpetual consolation.'

This was a strong-minded view of the case which Mrs. Dulcimer could by no means understand. It seemed to remove Beatrix further away from her. But then she had always been able to get on better with Bella than with Beatrix.

'You are not without friends, Beatrix, and advisers in this hour of trouble,' she said, encouragingly.

And then she told Beatrix about the two lawyers to whom the Vicar and his curate had written.

'Strange, was it not, that Cyril and my husband should both think of the same thing?'

'Very strange,' said Beatrix, deeply thoughtful.

'You see, my dear, the important question is, where did your father get the laudanum?'

'Oh, I think I know that,' answered Beatrix.

'You know, and did not tell the coroner? How very foolish!'

'I did not think of it yesterday. I could think of nothing. I felt as if I had lost myself in some hideous dream. But this morning, in my mother's room—I am free to go into my mother's room now—the idea occurred to me. It must have been there my poor father found the laudanum.'

'How do you know that?' asked Mrs. Dulcimer, eagerly.

Beatrix described her former visit to her mother's room, and how she had found a medicine chest there, and in the medicine chest a bottle half full of laudanum.

'I looked at the bottle this morning,' she said, 'and it was empty.'

'And your father was found lying dead in that room. Nothing can be clearer,' exclaimed Mrs. Dulcimer. 'The coroner ought to be communicated with immediately. How glad Clement will be! This will stop people's mouths.'

'What people?' asked Beatrix.

'Those horrid people who are always ready to think the worst of their neighbours. , I shall go back to the Vicarage at once. Clement ought to know without a moment's delay. How I wish you could eat your Christmas dinner with us, poor child! Kenrick has come back, looking so handsome, and so full of Culverhouse Castle. What a noble old place it must be! and what a pity he cannot afford to live in it!'

Beatrix did not hear a word about Culverhouse Castle.

'Cyril will be with you too, I suppose?' she said presently.

'No; it's extremely tiresome. Poor Cyril has one of his bad headaches, and says his only chance of getting through his evening duty is to keep quietly at home between the services. I feel quite annoyed. We have such a superb turkey. Rebecca chose it at Moyle's farm six weeks ago. It was a great fierce creature, and flew at her like a tiger when she went into the poultry-yard. Well, good-bye, dear. Pray keep up your spirits. Clement will be so glad to know about the laudanum.'

Beatrix sat alone, till the twilight gathered

round her, thinking of Cyril. To-day, for the first
time, she thought of her own position, which was
assuredly a horrible one. But she contemplated
it without a shadow of fear. Bella's speech yesterday, Mrs. Dulcimer's hints to-day, had shown
her that—in their minds at least—it seemed possible that people might suspect her of being her
father's murderer. There were people who would
think that she, to whom crime seemed as far off
as the stars, had blossomed all at once into the
most deliberate and vilest of criminals. Could
this really be so? Were there people capable
of believing such a thing? Why was not Cyril
near her in this hour of doubt and trouble? Mrs
Dulcimer came with her good-natured attempts at
consolation; but he, her natural consoler, held
himself aloof, now, when there was no one to bar
the door against him. Was it delicacy that kept
him away? Yes, possibly. He might consider
it an outrage against that silent master of the
house to cross his threshold unbidden.

'By and by, after the funeral, he will come,' she
thought.

He had entered the house yesterday as one of the public. She had seen him in the hall, but he had either not seen her, or had not chosen to recognise her. These things were bitter to her, but she fancied there must be some wise meaning in his conduct which she could not fathom.

'But he might at least have written to me,' she thought, piteously.

Bella came home from the Park by and by, full of the history of her day, trying to change the current of Beatrix's thoughts by talking briskly of all that had happened in the Piper *ménage*. Mr. Piper had been wonderfully kind, and had insisted upon the brougham being brought out to take her back to the Water House.

'I have no doubt the coachman hates me for bringing him out this damp evening,' said Bella, 'but Mr. Piper would not let me come any other way. "What's the use of having 'osses eating their heads off, and a parcel of idle fellers standing about chewing straw?" he said. "It 'll do 'em good to 'ave a turn."'

'How is poor Mrs. Piper?' Beatrix asked. languidly.

'Not any better. She had to dine in her own room. It was dreadful to see all those children stuffing turkey and pudding and mince pies, and making themselves spectacles of gluttony at dessert, without a thought of their poor mother, whose last Christmas Day was passing by—for I really don't think Mrs. Piper can live to see another Christmas.'

'Then you dined alone with Mr. Piper and the children?' inquired Beatrix, in the same listless tone.

'Not quite alone. Miss Coyle was there.'

Miss Coyle was a maiden lady of intense gentility, who possessed a small annuity—bestowed on her by the head of the house of Coyle, which was supposed to be a family of distinction—and who inhabited one of the prettiest cottages in Little Yafford—a rustic bower with a porch of green trellis-work, curtained with clematis and woodbine. The cottage was so small that a single friend dropping in to tea filled it to overflowing, insomuch that the small servant could hardly turn the corner of the parlour door with the tea-tray. This smallness Miss Coyle found economical. She visited a great deal in Little Yafford, and was not called upon to exercise any hospitality in return.

'With my poor little place it would be ridiculous to talk about giving parties,' she used to say, 'but if my friends will drop in upon me any afternoon they will always find a good cup of tea.'

Thus Miss Coyle contrived to cry quits with the best people in Little Yafford at the cost of a cup of tea. Even Mrs. Dulcimer—who prided herself upon the superiority of her tea—confessed that Miss Coyle excelled as a tea maker, and would condescend to drop in at the cottage once in a way on a hot summer afternoon, when the roads were ankle-deep in dust, and seemed longer than usual. Miss Coyle had not only tea to offer for the refreshment of the body, but she generally had some scrap of news for the entertainment of her visitor's mind. She was a wonderful woman in this way, and seemed always to be the first to know everything that occurred in Little Yafford, as if she had been the centre of an invisible telegraphic system.

'Oh, Miss Coyle was there, was she?' said Beatrix.

'Yes, she has been at the Park a good deal since the beginning of Mrs. Piper's illness. She goes to sit with poor Mrs. Piper almost every afternoon, and they talk of the wickedness of servants. Miss Coyle's father kept seven servants—four indoor and three outdoor. I have heard her describe them all, again and again. They seem to have been models; but Miss Coyle said they belonged to a race that has disappeared off the face of the earth—like the Drift people, or the poor Swiss creatures who lived in the lakes. You may imagine how lively it is to hear Miss Coyle and Mrs. Piper bewailing the iniquities of the present race.'

'Did Miss Coyle speak about my father—or me?' asked Beatrix, with an anxious look.

She remembered meeting Miss Coyle at the Vicarage two or three times, and she had a vague notion that if this lady had assisted at a memorable scene, when the sinless among the crowd were bidden to cast the first stone, she would assuredly have been ready with her pebble.

Bella looked embarrassed at the question.

'They did talk a little,' she faltered. 'Mr. Piper

and Miss Coyle. You know how vulgar and coarse he is—and I'm afraid she is not so good-natured as she pretends to be. But you must not be unhappy about anything such people can say.'

'Do you think I am going to make myself unhappy about it? Do you suppose I care what such people say or think of me?" exclaimed Beatrix, irritably.

'You must not imagine that they said anything very bad, dear,' said Bella, soothingly.

'I shall not imagine anything about them—their remarks are perfectly indifferent to me.'

'Of course, dear. What need you care what anybody says—or thinks—with your fortune? You can look down upon the world.'

'With my fortune!' echoed Beatrix, scornfully. 'I do not know whether I have sixpence belonging to me in this world, and I do not very much care. Indeed, I think I would just as soon be without fortune. I should find out what the world was like then.'

'Ah!' sighed Bella, 'you would see it "the seamy side without." It is a very rough world on the wrong side, I assure you.'

Beatrix did not answer. She was wondering how it would be if her father had left his estates away from her. If she were to find herself standing in the bleak hard world, penniless as the beggarmaid chosen by King Cophetua! Would Cyril, her king, in her mind 'the one pre-eminent man upon earth, would he, the true and noble lover, heedless of fortune, descend from his high estate to win her? She could not doubt that it would be so. Wealth or poverty could make no difference in him.

The weary week dragged slowly to its dull dark end. There was a stately funeral, solitary as the life of the dead man had been, for the mourners were but two—Mr. Scratchell, the agent, and Mr. Namby, the village doctor. But the escutcheoned hearse and nodding plumes, the huge Flemish horses with their manes combed reverse ways, the empty black carriages, the hired mourners, cloaked and scarved, and struggling heroically to impart a strangeness of expression to features which were familiar to the populace in every-day life—one of these venal followers being only too well known as a drunken carpenter, and another as a cobbler skilled in his art, but notorious for a too free use of the fire-irons in the correction of his wife and children—these trappings and suits of woe were not wanting. All that the most expensive undertaker in Great Yafford could devise to do honour to the dead was done; and Little Yafford, draining the dregs of its Christmas cup of dissipation, felt that Squire Harefield's funeral made an appropriate finish to the festivities of the season. The weather had changed; the bare barren fields were lightly powdered with snow, the black ridge of moorland was sharply cut against a bright blue sky.

'It's an outing, anyhow,' said the people of Little Yafford, and there was a good deal of extra liquor consumed at small wayside beerhouses after the funeral.

In the course of that afternoon the will was produced by Mr. Scratchell, who had drawn it, and who knew where to look for it. Nothing could be simpler or more decided. It had been executed nine years before, and, with the exception of legacies to old servants, and five hundred pounds to Mr. Scratchell, it left everything to Beatrix. Mr.

Dulcimer was made joint executor with Mr. Scratchell, and Beatrix's sole guardian in the event of her father dying while she was under age.

Two days later came the adjourned inquiry before the coroner. This time Beatrix Harefield's interests were watched by the lawyer from London, a little dark man, with heavy eyebrows and a hard mouth, a defender who inspired Beatrix with a nameless horror, although she could but be grateful to Cyril Culverhouse for his forethought in procuring her such skilled service. Mrs. Dulcimer had harped upon the curate's thoughtfulness in sending for one of the cleverest men in London to protect her dear Beatrix from the possibilities of evil.

'It was very kind of him,' Beatrix said somewhat constrainedly, 'but I would much rather have dispensed with the London lawyer—or any lawyer.'

'My dearest Beatrix, Mr. Dulcimer and Cyril must understand the exigencies of the case far better than you can, and both are agreed that the inquest cannot be too carefully watched on your behalf. If you only knew the dreadful things people say ' ——

Beatrix's marble cheek could grow no paler than

it had been in all the sorrowful days since her father's death, but a look of sharpest pain came into her face.

'Mrs. Dulcimer, do people think that I murdered my father?' she asked suddenly.

'My love,' cried the Vicar's wife, startled by this plain question, 'how can you suggest anything so horrible?'

'You suggested it, when you spoke of people saying dreadful things about me.'

'My dear Beatrix, I only meant to say that the world is very censorious. People are always ready to say cruel things—about the most innocent persons. It was so in David's time even. See how often he alludes to the malice and injustice of his enemies.'

Beatrix said no more, but, when Mrs. Dulcimer had left her, she sat for a long time with her face hidden in her clasped hands, in blank tearless grief.

'I see now why he shuns me,' she said to herself. 'He believes that I poisoned my father.'

Beatrix was one of the first witnesses examined at the adjourned inquest.

She made her statement about the medicine chest in her mother's room, and the empty laudanum bottle, simply and briefly.

'Why did you not mention this before?' asked the coroner.

'I forgot it.'

'What! could you forget a fact of such importance? You found your father dead in that very room, and you forgot the existence of a medicine chest, which, according to your statement of to-day, contained the poison by which he died.'

'The fact did not occur to me at the previous examination,' Beatrix answered firmly.

Her manner and bearing were curiously different from what they had been on the previous occasion. She was deadly pale, but firm as a rock. That firmness of hers, the calm distinctness of her tones, the proud carriage of her beautiful head, impressed the coroner and jury strongly, but not favourably. They had been more ready to sympathize with her a week ago, when she had stood before them trembling, and bowed down by her distress.

The medicine chest was brought from the late

Mrs. Harefield's room. There was the bottle as Beatrix had described it—an empty bottle which had obviously contained laudanum.

'Do you know if your mother was in the habit of taking laudanum?' asked the coroner.

'I know very little about her. All that I can remember of her is like a dream.'

Mr. Namby was re-examined upon this question of the laudanum.

He remembered that Mrs. Harefield had suffered from neuralgic pains in the head and face during the last year of her residence at the Water House. She had complained to him, and he had prescribed for her, not successfully. He was of opinion that the Water House was too much on a level with the river. He would not go so far as to say the house was damp, but he was sure it was not dry. It was not unlikely that Mrs. Harefield would resort to laudanum as a palliative. He had never given her laudanum.

Peacock, the butler, was examined. He remembered Mrs. Harefield complaining of pain in the head and face. It was called tic-dollerer. He fancied the name meant something like toothache, independent of teeth. As he understood it you might have tic-dollerer anywheres. He remembered being in Great Yafford with the carriage one day when Mrs. Harefield told him to go into a chemist's shop and ask for some laudanum. He got a small quantity in a bottle. Mrs. Harefield used often to drive into Great Yafford. Sometimes he went on the box with the coachman— sometimes not. He knew that she had a medicine chest in her room. He had heard Chugg, the young woman who waited on her, say that she took sleeping draughts.

The jury agreed upon their verdict, after some deliberation.

Mr. Harefield had died from the effects of laudanum, but by whom administered there was no evidence to show.

CHAPTER VI.

BELLA'S REVENGE.

THE blinds were drawn up at the Water House, and the wintry sun shone upon the empty rooms. Miss Scales had come back to her charge, leaving that provoking old lady in Devonshire still undecided whether to live or die, 'making it so very perplexing as to one's choice of a winter dress when one might be called upon at any moment to go into mourning,' Miss Scales complained to her Devonshire acquaintance, when discussing her aunt's weak-minded oscillation.

But now there was no further difficulty about the mourning question. For Mr. Harefield, her employer of fifteen years, Miss Scales could not assume too deep a sable, especially when the sable would naturally be provided and paid for by her dearest Beatrix.

Banbury and Banbury's forewoman came to the

Water House with boxes of crape and rolls of bombazine, and the governess and her pupil were measured for garments of unutterable woe.

And now, at nineteen, Beatrix found herself on the threshold of a new life, a life of supreme independence. Wealth, and liberty to do what she pleased with it, were hers. Mr. Dulcimer was likely to prove the ˉmost indulgent of guardians; Mr. Scratchell was subservient to the last degree, his sole anxiety being to retain his position, and to ingratiate himself and his family in Miss Harefield's favour.

'If Mrs. Scratchell can be useful in any way, pray command her,' said the village lawyer. 'She will be only too proud to serve you, Miss Harefield, but she would be the last to obtrude her services.'

'I do not think you need entertain any apprehensions as to Miss Harefield's being properly taken care of, Mr. Scratchell,' Miss Scales remarked, stiffly. 'She has Mr. Dulcimer—and she has ME.'

Mr. Scratchell rumpled the scanty bristles at the top of his bald head, and felt himself snubbed.

'Neither Mrs. Scratchell nor myself would wish to obtrude ourselves,' he said, 'but Miss Harefield being fond of Bella might like to make use of Mrs. Scratchell. She is a very clever manager, and might put Miss Harefield in the right way with her servants.'

'Miss Harefield's servants know their duties, and do not require managing, Mr. Scratchell. I should be very sorry to live in a household where the servants had to be managed. The bare idea implies a wrong state of things.'

'Well,' exclaimed Mr. Scratchell, testily, 'I don't want to press myself or my family upon Miss Harefield—although I am joint executor with Mr. Dulcimer, and had the honour to enjoy her father's confidence for five-and-thirty years. I should be very sorry to be intrusive. And there's Bella, she has made a very long stay here, and she's wanted badly elsewhere. If Miss Harefield is agreeable she had better come home.'

'She must do as she likes,' Beatrix answered, listlessly. 'I am a very dull companion for her.'

'Dear Beatrix, yon know I love to be with you,'

murmured Bella, in her affectionate way, ' but I
think I ought to go home, as papa says. Poor
Mrs. Piper is so ill, and the young Pipers get more
troublesome every day. Their holidays are too
trying for her. I believe I ought to resume my
duties.'

'I am sure you ought,' said her father, who was
bursting to assert his independence. He did
not mind how subservient he made himself to
Beatrix, but he was not going to knuckle under to
Miss Scales. ' I met Mr. Piper in the village yesterday, and he told me the house was all at sixes and
sevens for want of you.'

Beatrix seemed indifferent as to whether Bella
went or stayed, so Miss Scratchell got her goods and
chattels together, and departed with her father, after
many loving embraces and pretty expressions of gratitude. Perhaps in the book of the recording angel
that parting kiss of Bella's went down in a particular
column devoted to such Judas kisses—that traitor
kiss of Darnley's, for instance, on the night of Rizzio's
assassination.

Bella went home with her father, looking slim

and pretty in her new black dress and bonnet, and
doing her best to soothe her parent's wrath with
sweet deprecating speeches. In the box which she
had just packed—to be brought home later—there
were many things that she had not taken to the
Water House, including a handsome black silk gown,
and innumerable trifles in the shape of gloves, collars,
and neck-ribbons; but there was one thing which
Miss Scratchell carried away in her pocket, and
which she held to be of more importance than all
her finery.

This was the sealed envelope which she had
found upon Mr. Harefield's writing-table. 'For
my daughter Beatrix.'

She took it from her pocket when she was
safely locked in her own room, secure from the
intrusion of the family herd. She sat with the
packet on her lap, thoughtfully contemplating it.

She had kept it more than a fortnight, and
had not broken the seal. She had been sorely
tempted to see what was inside the envelope, but
had resisted the temptation. To open it would be
a crime, she had told herself, and she made a kind

of virtue of this self-denial. All she wanted was
to keep the document. She had made up her
mind that this sealed packet contained the key
to the mystery of Christian Harefield's death. So
long as the seal remained unbroken that death
would remain a mystery. No one would know
whether it was suicide or murder; and this uncertainty would hang like a cloud over Beatrix.

This was Isabella Scratchell's revenge. That
pink and white prettiness of hers was not incompatible with the capacity to seize an opportunity
and to persevere in an inexorable hatred.

'She has beauty and wealth, and a good old
name,' thought Bella; 'but so long as her father's
death remains unexplained she will hardly have
the love of Cyril Culverhouse.'

Bella had heard enough from Mr. Piper and
Miss Coyle on Christmas Day to know very well
which way opinion was drifting in Little Yafford.
It was a settled thing already in the minds of a
good many deep thinkers, and profound students
of human nature as exhibited in the weekly
papers, that Beatrix Harefield knew more about

her father's death than anybody else. The very
horror of the idea that her hand had put the
poison in his way gave it a morbid attraction for
tea-table conversation. There was a growing
opinion that the coroner's jury had done less
than their duty in returning an open verdict.

'The verdict would have been very different
if Miss Harefield had been a labouring man's
daughter,' said Miss Coyle, who had more to say
on this subject than any one else, and who was
always uncompromising in her opinions.

Bella was not sorry to leave the Water House,
though home looked a little more squalid and un-
tidy than usual, after the subdued splendour of
Miss Harefield's mansion. She had not been able
to feel at her ease with Beatrix during this last
visit. Even to her essentially false nature there
was some effort required to preserve a demeanour
of unvarying sweetness towards a person she de-
tested. The old Adam was in danger of breaking
out now and then. Between Beatrix and herself
there stood the shadowy image of Cyril Culverhouse; and there were moments when Bella could

not quite command her looks, however sweetly she might attune her voice. And now that Miss Scales was on the scene, with eyes which saw everything, Bella felt that the veneer of affection might be too thin to hide the hardness of the wood underneath it.

So Bella resumed the monotonous order of her home life, breakfasted at eight, and presented herself at the Park upon the stroke of nine, where the Piper children, clustering round the newly-lighted fire in the schoolroom, hated her for her punctuality. But she knew that if the children disapproved, Mr. Piper approved, for he generally looked out of the dining-room, newspaper in hand, to give her a friendly nod of welcome.

'Good little girl, always up to time,' he said; 'those are the 'abits that make success in life. That was Brougham's way. He might be hard at it, drinking and dissipating far into the small hours, but he was always up to time in the morning. Cobbett was never too late for an appointment in his life. Those are the men for my money.'

'How is dear Mrs. Piper?'

'Well, I think the missus is a trifle better this morning; but she mends very slow, poor soul. I don't believe the doctors can do much for her.'

Bella sighed, and shook her head sadly, and then went tripping upstairs to the schoolroom, leaving Mr. Piper standing at the dining-room door looking after her.

'A pretty little girl,' he said to himself, 'neatly finished off, like a well-made carriage, or an English watch. No scamping about the workmanship. Poor Moggie never had as pretty a figure as that, though she was a trim-built lass when she and me was courting.'

One day, when Bella had finished the weary round of lessons, and had nearly addled her brains in the endeavour to awaken Brougham's sluggish mind to the difference between the active and the passive voices of the verb 'amo,' she paid her usual visit to Mrs. Piper, and found that lady in tears over a book of sermons.

'Dear Mrs. Piper,' cried Bella, with a sympathizing look, 'have you been feeling worse this morning?'

'No, Bella, bodily I'm much the same, but I've been giving way. It's very wrong of me, I know, but there are times when I do give way. To-day I haven't been able to feel quite happy in my mind. I don't feel my calling and election sure. I don't feel myself sealed with the seal of righteousness. I don't feel myself a chosen vessel.'

'You to say this, dear Mrs. Piper! you who have been so good!'

'If goodness lies in reading sermons, Bella—and in constant attendance at chapel or church, I may say I have done my duty. We were chapel people in Great Yafford, you know, my dear; but when we came to the Park, Piper and me both felt that chapel wasn't consistent. Such a house as this, and seven indoor servants don't accord with chapel—so we became Church of England people, as you know, Bella; but I don't think I ever felt so sure of salvation since. Mr. Dulcimer is a fine preacher, but he has never given me assurance of salvation. No more has Mr. Culverhouse, though his sermons go through my heart like an arrow. Church is very nice, Bella, and I don't deny that the bonnets and general appearance of the congregation bear a higher stamp, but chapel is the place to make a sinner comfortable in his mind. Since I have been confined to these rooms, Bella, and my mind has been taken off the housekeeping, I feel there is something wanting. I should so like to have a little talk with Mr. Mowler, of Zion Chapel, our old minister. I know that he would understand me, and——'

'Not better than Mr. Culverhouse,' cried Bella, eagerly. 'You don't know how good he is, how tender of one's feelings, how sympathetic. I have visited among his poor, and have heard him talk to sick people. He is an angel of consolation. Do let him come and sit with you, and read or talk to you.'

'I shouldn't mind,' said Mrs. Piper, 'but I'm afraid his views are not evangelical enough for me.'

'I don't know much about his views, but I know it is beautiful to hear him talk. Shall I ask him to come this afternoon?'

'You may, if you like, Bella, if you can take such a liberty. I want some one to strengthen my hope of redemption. There was a time when I believed myself one of the elect, but sitting alone up here my thoughts have dwelt upon many things that never troubled me when I had the free use of my limbs. I begin to think that church-going and pious reading may not be all in all. I have been like Martha, troubled about many things. I have worried myself too much about the things of this world. I have not considered the lilies of the field, or the birds of the air. I have not been grateful enough for my many blessings, or kind enough to my neighbours. Providence has showered wealth upon me and Piper, and I'm afraid we might have made a better use of it.'

'I am sure you have been kind to me,' said Bella.

'I might have been kinder. I'm afraid I've only been kind because you've been useful to me. I suppose there's some spots and stains in the lives of the best of us; but my life seems to me all blackened over with weeds and foul spots when I look back upon it. Oh, Bella, to think of the many things I might have done! There's my own blood relations! I've kept them at arm's length, only because I thought their clothes and manners would be a blot upon this house. I've been a slave to this house, and the slavery has killed me. I was a happier woman when we lived in the Great Yafford Road, and when I helped to make the beds and dust the rooms every morning, and made my own pastry and cakes. That was what I was born for, Bella, not to be cheated and made light of by a parcel of stuck-up servants.'

'I shall pass Mr. Culverhouse's lodgings as I go home,' said Bella. 'I'll ask him to come and chat with you.'

'You may, my dear; though I don't feel that I shall get the same comfort from him that I should from Mr. Mowler.'

Bella walked briskly through the Park, reflecting on the foolishness of human nature. Here was Mrs. Piper, to whom had been given such great prosperity, and who had made so little use of her advantages, frittering away life upon trivial anxieties, and missing the chance of happiness. She looked along the fine old avenue, and thought how much grandeur and importance a sensible young woman like herself might have derived from such surroundings. But on poor Mrs. Piper all these good things had been thrown away. That poor dull bit of agate looked ridiculous in the splendid setting which would have been quite in harmony with a shining little gem like Bella Scratchell. It was a clear bright winter day, the sky blue, the moor a warm purple, the leafless woods lightly powdered with snow, white patches lying here and there among the dark trunks of oak and elm. Bella walked quickly through the Park and along the high road leading to the village.

CHAPTER VII.

MINE OWN FAMILIAR FRIEND.

THE house in which Mr. Culverhouse lodged was on the outskirts of Little Yafford, a comfortable square cottage, with a long slip of garden between the dusty high road and the shady green porch, a garden, where in summer tall white lilies, bush roses, double stocks, and clove carnations grew abundantly in long narrow borders, edged with a thick fence of irreproachable box. Miss Coyle's model cottage, with its green venetians and verandah, shining window-panes, and general appearance of having come out of a toy-shop, stood on the opposite side of the way, and even the perfection of Miss Coyle's miniature garden did not put to shame the neatness of Mrs. Pomfret's larger domain. Mrs. Pomfret was pew opener, and had occupied that post of honour ever since her marriage with Mr. Pomfret, the sexton. Mr. Pomfret was in his

grave, and the excellent management whereby
Mrs. Pomfret contrived to make so good a figure
and wear such spotless caps, upon the profits of
opening pews and letting lodgings, was a wonder
to the housekeepers of Little Yafford. If Mrs.
Pomfret had been disposed to impart the recipe
by which she had done these things, she could
have told it in two words, and those two words
would have been, temperance and industry.

The first of the snowdrops had not yet pierced
the dark mould, but the shining leaves of bay
and berberis, and holly and laurel brightened the
long slip of garden. Bella opened the little gate
hesitatingly, as if there were something awful in
the act. She felt that she was making a desperate plunge in calling upon Cyril Culverhouse;
but Mrs. Piper's sad condition was her justifica-
tion.

She had seen him very seldom since that evening at the Vicarage, when Mrs. Dulcimer forced
him to a revealment of his feelings. It was a
memory that had lost none of its bitterness with
the passage of time; and yet Bella yearned to

see him, and was glad of an excuse for approaching him.

Mrs. Pomfret opened the door, and saluted Miss Scratchell with a surprised curtsey. She was a thin little woman, dressed in perpetual black, and the stiffest of widow's caps, which framed her small hard face with a broad band of starched muslin that would have been trying to the countenance of a Hebe, and which made Mrs. Pomfret's complexion look like unpolished mahogany. But Mrs. Pomfret did not wear a widow's cap because it was becoming, or comfortable. She wore it as a badge of respectability.

Mr. Culverhouse was at home. He opened the parlour door at the sound of Bella's voice, and looked out.

'Is it you, Miss Scratchell? How do you do?' he said, with calm friendliness. 'Pray come in. Is Mary Smithers worse? Have you come to fetch me to her? I am afraid she has not many days to live.'

Bella's eyes were rapturously devouring the

room. His room. It looked like the room of a
gentleman and a student. Those books, piled row
above row in the shabby old bookcase, were his,
of course. There was his open desk upon the
table. His hat and cane were on a side table.
There was no disorder, nothing squalid or un-
sightly.

'No, I have not come from Mary Smithers,'
said Bella. 'I want to enlist your sympathy for
poor Mrs. Piper.'

And then Bella explained the sad condition
into which Mrs. Piper had fallen, how in the
hour of sickness her soul hankered after the
strong meat of the Baptist chapel where she
had worshipped in her youth, and how she would
assuredly seek for comfort from Mr. Mowler,
unless the Church of England came to her
rescue.

'I should have asked Mr. Dulcimer to see her,
said Bella, 'only, dear and good as he is, I do not
think he is earnest enough to give hope and comfort to a person in her situation. If you would
be so kind as to call upon her.'

'I will go immediately.'

'Oh, how good you are!' cried Bella, her eyes shining with enthusiasm.'

Mr. Culverhouse reddened. That little gush of flattery reminded him uncomfortably of his conversation with Mrs. Dulcimer.

'There is no goodness in a clergyman trying to do his duty, any more than in a baker carrying round his loaves,' he said, coolly.

He put on his overcoat, and took up his hat and cane, and he and Bella went out together. That cool tone of his wounded her keenly.

'Are you still with Miss Harefield?' he said, at the garden gate.

Bella gave him an icy look. The mention of that name was a second stab.

'No, I have left her some time.'

Cyril saw the look, and perceived the unfriendliness in the tone. He put down both to a wrong cause. His face was full of care as he walked to the Park.

'Mine own familiar friend,' he said to himself, sadly.

Bella found Mrs. Piper in better spirits on the following day.

'Oh, my dear, Mr. Culverhouse is a saint!' she exclaimed, when Bella had seated herself by the invalid's sofa. 'He has given me great comfort. He has not flattered me, you know, my dear. He does not deny that I have misused my advantages. I have not done all that I might for my fellow-creatures. I have taken too much thought of the letter, and not followed the spirit. Oh, he is a good man.'

'Is he not?' cried Bella, delighted at this praise.

'I shall ask Piper to subscribe double to all his charities. We have subscribed 'andsome, but we have done it because it was in keeping with this house to have our names stand out well in the subscription lists. I should like to give Mr. Culverhouse a sum of money, unbeknown to anybody, that he might lay it out to my advantage, where neither moth nor rust doth corrupt, nor thieves break through and steal. I don't think I shall ever worry myself about the butcher's book any more, Bella. · Sickness has opened my eyes to the vanity of such petty cares.'

Bella sighed, thinking of the harassed house-keeper at home. For the rich manufacturer's wife such small cares were vanity, but for Mrs. Scratchell they were the serious things of life. With her it was not so much the question as to whether she had been cheated out of a pound or two of meat, but whether she could honestly afford a Sunday joint for her children.

'Mr. Culverhouse said he would call again soon,' said Mrs. Piper, and this gave Bella the hope of meeting him at the Park some morning.

Before the week ended that hope was realized, and with its realization came another turning-point in Bella's life—a meeting of roads, as in the choice of Hercules, when a man or woman goes to the right or left, choosing the broad smooth highway of inclination, or the narrow thorny path of duty, according as passion or conscience is ruler of fate.

Bella had stopped later than usual one afternoon, Horne Tooke and Brougham having been stupid and rebellious to a degree that necessitated an exemplary punishment in the shape of three Latin verbs, and Elizabeth Fry having exhibited a deeper density than usual as to the intervals of the minor scale. These difficulties had prolonged the morning's lessons until after the children's dinner, and it was nearly four o'clock when Bella, thoroughly wearied out, put on her neat little black bonnet and bade her sullen pupils good-bye.

'I hope you don't bear malice, Elizabeth,' she said at parting. 'I am obliged to be a little severe about those scales. It's for your good, you know. It can't make any difference to me whether you know how to change the major into minor.'

'And I'm sure I don't see that it can make any difference to me,' protested the injured Elizabeth. 'I am not going to be a governess.'

'Very fortunate for you, my dear,' answered Bella, lightly, 'for if you were obliged to get your living in that way, you would have to be one of the poor things who don't object to make themselves generally useful; which means that they are to make all their pupils' clothes, and work a great deal harder than housemaids.'

And, with this arrow shot over Elizabeth Fry's dull head, Bella pulled on her gloves and departed,

In the hall she met Cyril going away. He greeted her with friendliness, and they went out into the wintry twilight together.

'I am glad you have been to see Mrs. Piper again,' said Bella, 'your visits have done her so much good.'

'I am very happy to hear that. She is a kindly, simple-hearted creature, sorely tried by prosperity, which is for some natures a harder ordeal than adversity.'

They walked on for some distance in silence, Bella looking thoughtfully at her companion, every now and then, speculating upon the causes of his absent manner and troubled face.

'I am afraid you have been working too hard lately, Mr. Culverhouse,' she said at last. 'You are looking ill and wearied.'

'I have been troubled in mind,' he answered. 'I am seldom any worse for what you call hard work— but I have had bitter anxieties since Christmas. Have you seen Miss Harefield lately?'

'No,' answered Bella, 'she has plenty of friends without me.'

'I do not think she has many friends—in Little Yafford.'

'She has the Dulcimers, who are devoted to her.'

'Mr. Dulcimer is her guardian, and executor to her father's will. I am sure he will do all that is right and kind.'

'Do you mean that Mrs. Dulcimer is not kind to Beatrix?' asked Bella, her heart beating fast and fiercely.

From the moment he mentioned Beatrix Harefield's name in the same breath with his own anxieties he had in a manner admitted his love for her.

'It is not in Mrs. Dulcimer's nature to be unkind,' said Cyril, 'but I fear she is not so warmly attached to Miss Harefield as she was a short time ago.'

'You think perhaps she has been influenced by things that have been said in Little Yafford,' suggested Bella, eagerly.

'I fear so.'

'I am very sorry for that. I pity Beatrix with all my heart. But deeply as I compassionate her wretched position, I hardly wonder that people should feel differently about her since her father's death.'

'Do you—her own familiar friend—suspect her of the most awful crime the mind of man can conceive?' exclaimed Cyril. 'She may well stand condemned in the eyes of strangers if her bosom friend believes her guilty.'

'Oh, Mr. Culverhouse, how can you suggest anything so horrible?' cried Bella.

'I looked to you for her defence,' he went on without heeding this ejaculation. 'The outside world might suspect her. I, even, who have seen much in her to admire—and love—but who have had no opportunity of knowing her thoroughly, I might waver in my judgment—might be weakly influenced by the evil thoughts of others; but you who have lived with her like a sister, you must know the very depth of her heart—surely you can rise up boldly and say that she could not do this hideous thing. It is not in her nature to become —no, I will not utter the loathsome word,' he cried, passionately.

Bella answered nothing. Cyril looked at her searchingly in the grey evening light. Her eyelids were lowered, her face was grave and troubled.

'What!' he exclaimed; 'not a word—not one word in defence of your friend?'

'What can I say?' faltered Bella, with an embarrassed air. 'Do you want me to tell you what I saw in that gloomy house? No, I had rather not say a word. Think me unkind, ungenerous if you like. I shall be silent about all things concerning Miss Harefield and her father.'

Cyril looked at her for a moment, with a countenance of blank despair. She saw the look, and it intensified her hatred of Beatrix.

'How he must have loved her!' she thought, 'but will he go on loving her in the face of a suspicion that is daily growing stronger?'

Outside the Park gates Cyril left her.

'I am going the other way,' he said, abruptly, and then he raised his hat and walked quickly along the high road that led away from Little Yafford.

'Where can he be going?' speculated Bella. 'I believe he only went that way to avoid me.'

It was not a promising commencement, but it seemed to Bella's scheming little mind that Cyril's affection, once weaned from Beatrix, would naturally turn to her. There was no one else in Little Yafford with any great pretensions to beauty, and a great many people had praised Bella's delicate prettiness. So long as he was devoted to Beatrix, Mr. Culverhouse would no doubt remain stone blind to the charms of Bella; but Beatrix once banished from his heart, there would be plenty of room there for a small person with smiling blue eyes and winning manners.

This was the hope that lured Bella onward upon the ugly road she had chosen for herself, while jealousy impelled her to do harm to her rival, even though that wrong might result in no gain to herself.

CHAPTER VIII.

CYRIL RENOUNCES LOVE AND FORTUNE.

CYRIL CULVERHOUSE was a miserable man. The woman he loved—the only woman he had ever loved—was free to become his wife, dowered with estates worth ten thousand a year, and yet he held himself aloof from her, and shrank from any act which should ratify in the present the tie that had bound them in the past. He, who should have been the first to console the fatherless girl in the hour of bereavement and desolation, to support and counsel her under the difficulties of sudden independence—he, whose heart yearned towards her in her loneliness, stood apart and allowed her to believe him cold and heartless. The struggle had been a hard one; but, after many troubled days and wakeful nights, he had made up his mind that it must be so. Beatrix and he could never go hand in hand along the path of life.

The cloud that hung over her young life might be a shadow which the light of truth would by and by dispel; but, until the truth should appear, broad and clear as sunlight, he could not take Beatrix Harefield to his heart, he could not bind his life with hers.

Did he believe her guilty of that last and worst of crimes, the murder of a father? Hardly. But he was not fully assured of her innocence. His mind had been racked with doubt—ever since that day of the inquest when he had stood in the doorway and watched her agonized face and listened to her faltering words. There is nothing that the human mind more unwillingly believes than a strange coincidence; and that coincidence of Miss Harefield's purchase of the laudanum within a week of her father's death by laudanum had been too much for Cyril's faith. Had his beloved been a penniless orphan, and no worldly gain to be had from loving her, he might have reconciled his doubt with his honour and married her, trusting to time for the elucidation of the mystery that now stained her young life with the taint of possible guilt. But in this

case there was too much for him to win—and
in every feeling that drew him to Beatrix he recognised a snare of Satan. Little by little he had
come to know that public opinion in Little Yafford
—and even in the neighbouring town of Great
Yafford—had condemned Beatrix Harefield. Every
detail of her conduct had been canvassed. Her
late appearance on the morning of her father's death
was taken as an evidence of guilt. She had feared
to face the catastrophe her crime had brought about,
and had feigned sleep to stave off the appalling
moment. Or she had simulated that heavy slumber
in order to support her story about the laudanum.
Her suggestion that her father should be sought for
in a certain room, and the fact that he was found
in that very room ; her lame story—obviously an
after thought—of the laudanum bottle in her mother's
room—all told against her. The fact that an empty
bottle had been found there proved nothing.
Beatrix had no doubt placed it where it was found.
There had been ample time for her to do so between
the first and second meetings of the coroner's jury.
Then as to motive ? Well, one need not look very

far for that, argued Little Yafford. Mr. Harefield had been a tyrant, and had made his daughter's life miserable. She saw in his death a release from his tyranny, with the assurance of wealth and independence. Everybody knew—thanks to Mrs. Dulcimer—how cruelly the wretched girl had been treated, even forbidden to visit the Vicarage, where she had always been so happy. And then there was that secret love affair which had been spoken about at the inquest. That would give a still stronger motive than her own wrongs. The more cultured inhabitants of Little Yafford, gentlemen who had dipped into old magazines and Annual Registers, quoted the case of Miss Blandy, an unfortunate young woman in the last century, who had given Henley-on-Thames, the place of her birth and residence, a classic fame by poisoning her father with ratsbane mixed in his water gruel.

Again, as to character. Everybody who was familiar with Miss Harefield—by meeting her occasionally in her drives and rides, or seeing her once a week at church—was aware that she was a girl of reserved and even melancholy temperament, from whom anything strange in conduct or morals might be expected. Then, again, she was of foreign extraction on the mother's side, and as such prone to crime. She was Italian, and with a natural leaning to poison and parricide. And again, those stock figures of the Borgia and Cenci were brought forward and contemplated shudderingly in the lurid glare of their guilt.

Some weak-minded persons clung to the idea that Mr. Harefield had taken an overdose of opium unwittingly, but this tame and uninteresting theory was scouted by the majority.

'If Miss Harefield had not been an heiress we should have heard a good deal more about her father's death,' said Miss Coyle, draining her ancestral teapot at one of her temperate symposia.

Miss Coyle was quite angry with the coroner for not having looked deeper into things. She spoke of him contemptuously as a hireling and a time-server.

Cyril Culverhouse knew what people thought about the woman he loved—for he loved her none the less because he held himself aloof from her. His

love was deathless. Innocent or guilty he must love
her to the end. He knew what people thought of
his beloved; he knew that even kindly Mrs. Dulcimer
shook her head, and shrank from familiar contact
with her husband's ward. There was no one in
Little Yafford except the Vicar who would take the
slandered girl by the hand and boldly demonstrate
his belief in her innocence. He, so easy-going on
most occasions, was firm as a rock here. He would
have Beatrix at his house, as often as she chose to
come there—although the all-powerful Rebecca
would hardly look civilly at her as she waited at
table—and although poor Mrs. Dulcimer was sorely
perplexed by her presence. Clement Dulcimer was
staunch, and defied his parishioners, whom he
stigmatised generally as a pack of venomous scandal-
mongers, whose uncultured minds, unable to appreciate the strong sound meat of literature, battened
upon carrion.

If Cyril could have had Mr. Dulcimer's faith he
would have had Mr. Dulcimer's courage. He was no
slave of other men's opinions, and would have
snapped his fingers in the face of Little Yafford, if

all had been well within. But there was the difficulty. That stricken face of Beatrix's, those wild
startled eyes—as he had seen them in the candle-lit
room at the Water House—haunted him like an evil
dream. He saw guilt and remorse in those troubled
looks—the fear of God and man. Had he been a
man who lived for himself alone, who had no higher
aim in life than his own happiness, Cyril Culverhouse might have stifled the voice of doubt, and listened only to love's pleading. But it was not so
with him—he had chosen a loftier kind of life, he
had given himself a loftier aim. He was to live for
others, and to make the lives of others better than
their own unaided weakness could make them. He,
who was to be the teacher and counsellor of others,
must be, so far as it is possible for humanity, spotless
in his life and in his surroundings. Could he marry
a wife of whom it could be said in one breath, 'She
was suspected of poisoning her father,' and in the
next, 'Yes, but she brought her husband ten thousand
a year'?

No. It was clear to him that this fatal cloud of
suspicion must make a life-long severance between

Beatrix and him. Love might have bridged the gulf, but honour and duty held him back. He had not seen Beatrix since her father's death, and he had made up his mind to leave Little Yafford without seeing her. His business was to announce his resolve in a manner that would give her the least pain possible; but he knew the blow would be hard to bear. He knew that she loved him with an intense and all-absorbing love.

'Oh, God, if she has sinned so deeply for the love of me,' he thought, in a moment of horror, finding himself suddenly on the edge of a black abyss of doubt, down which he dared not look, 'if to bring about our union she has done this hideous thing! But no, I will not believe her guilty. I will pity and deplore her position, the victim of groundless suspicion. If I dare not sacrifice my duty to my love, I will at least believe her innocent.'

He remembered that little speech of hers during their chance meeting on the moor, a speech that had shocked and revolted him at the time, and had been a painful recollection to him afterwards.

'Is it wicked to wish for my father's death?'

Did not that question imply that she had already committed the sin? Was it possible that the wicked wish, nursed and cherished, had culminated in the fatal act? The doubt tortured him.

He had wavered for some weeks, not quite clear in his own mind what step he ought to take, hoping that some new piece of evidence, some detail in the story of Christian Harefield's death, might place the whole business in a new light, and demonstrate Beatrix's innocence. But Mr. Harefield had been dead a month, the first snowdrops were lifting their heads out of the dark borders, the robins were singing sweetly in the lengthening afternoons, and nothing had been discovered to improve Miss Harefield's position in the eyes of Little Yafford. Nay rather, slander had grown and intensified with discussion, and people who had timorously hinted their doubts three weeks ago, now boldly declared their conviction of the young lady's guilt.

'How she can live in that big lonely house, with no one but her governess for company, is more than I can understand,' said Miss Coyle; 'she must be dreadfully hardened.'

'Something more will come out before long, you may depend upon it,' said Mrs. Pomfret, the pew-opener, to her Sunday afternoon gossips over the black crockery teapot, with a sphinx squatting on the lid.

This was the general opinion. Everybody was waiting for something to come out. The servants had doubtless been paid to hold their tongues—dark facts had been kept back by bribery. But the truth would come out sooner or later—even if Mr. Hare-field's ghost had to walk, like the elder Hamlet.

'It may be a very long time, but it will all come out sooner or later,' said Mr. Tudway, an old bachelor retired from the button trade, a great reader of magazines and annual registers, who knew all about Miss Blandy, and talked learnedly of Lucretia Borgia and Beatrice Cenci. 'Look at Eliza Fenning.'

'Ah!' sighed Miss Coyle. 'Very true.'

She had the vaguest recollection of Eliza Fenning, as associated uncomfortably with beefsteak dumplings, and hanged in consequence of the association, but she was not going to exhibit her igno-

rance before Mr. Tudway, who was disagreeably
self-satisfied on the strength of his stray paragraphs,
and unconsidered scraps of information.

Beatrix Harefield was slow to discover the
current of public feeling. The shock of her
father's death left her for a little while apathetic to
all smaller emotions, and when that apathy wore
off she had a new and pressing grief in Cyril's
abandonment. Her new sense of liberty brought
her no happiness—no desire to taste the sweets of
freedom, or to exchange the gloom and solitude of
the Water House for brighter scenes. If her independence did not bring Cyril to her side it brought
nothing. Wealth, power, liberty, were valueless
without him.

The slow days went by, and she waited for
her lover to make some sign. At first she was
inclined to impute his conduct to a restraining
delicacy, but as time went on a horrible fear
began to take hold of her aching heart. He was
purposely avoiding her. She had spent her Sunday evenings at the Vicarage. Kenrick had been
there, but never Cyril. She had heard Mrs. Dul-

'What a hermit you are growing'! said Kenrick. 'You hardly ever come to the Vicarage now.'

'I have so much to do else where.'

'But on Sunday evenings,' suggested Kenrick, helping himself to a pipe from the neat arrangement of meerschaums and briar-woods on the mantelpiece. 'Surely you could spare an hour or two after evening service for social intercourse. That is always the pleasantest time at the Vicarage.'

'I have been engaged even on Sunday evenings.'

'Yes, of course ; for a man who visits the poor there must be always an engagement. That kind of thing has no limit. Poor people like to be read to and talked to and compassionated. You can't suppose they would ever say, " Hold, enough!" But you ought to have some consideration for your own health and spirits. You are looking ill and depressed.'

'I am not ill, but I plead guilty to feeling depressed.'

'What is the trouble ?'

'I have made up my mind to leave this place—

dear as it is to me.   I am going to write to Mr. Dulcimer this evening to tell him my intention.'

'You must be mad,' cried Kenrick.   'Leave
Little Yafford, just when fortune is ready to pour
her favours into your lap—just when Miss Harefield is free to be your wife.   You must be mad,
Cyril.'

'No, I have been sorely perplexed, but I am not
mad.   I have deliberately weighed this question.
Beatrix Harefield is to me the one perfect woman—
the only woman I can ever love,—but I cannot ask
her to be my wife.'

'Why not, in heaven's name ? '

'I had rather not enter into my feelings on that
point.'

'Do you mean that you, a reasonable man, with
eyes of your own and a mind of your own to see
and judge with, are going to be led and ruled by
the petty slanderers of Little Yafford; malicious
creatures who envy Miss Harefield her ten thousand a year, and would like to think—or at any
rate to make others think—that she jumped into
fortune by crime ? '

'I despise slanderers and evil speakers,' said Cyril, 'but my wife must be spotless.'

'Yes, in your own eyes and in the sight of heaven. It can matter to you very little what Little Yafford thinks of her.'

'To me individually nothing—to my office a great deal. The wife of a priest must be above suspicion—her name and fame must be unshadowed.'

'Abandon your office, then. You can afford to do it if you marry a woman with ten thousand a year.'

Cyril turned upon the speaker with eyes that flashed angrily across a cloud of gray smoke.

'Kenrick, can you believe for one moment that I took that office as a means of living, or that the gain of wealth or happiness would tempt me to surrender it? I should think myself a new Judas if I could turn my back upon my Master to marry the woman I love.'

'Keep your office, then, and marry her all the same. Live down this slander. Stand up bravely before the world with your wife by your side, and let men say the worst they can of you. Your life and hers will be your answer.'

'They would say I had married her because she has ten thousand a year,' said Cyril. 'I should do no good with her money. It would turn to withered leaves in my keeping. No, I love her—shall love her to the end—innocent or guilty—but I will not link my life with hers. Every hour of life would be a struggle between love and doubt.'

'Innocent or guilty!' echoed Kenrick. 'I see you are as bad as the rest. I should not have thought that possible. You have quite made up your mind then, Cyril. You abandon all hope of winning Miss Harefield?'

'Entirely.'

'So be it,' said Kenrick. 'Then let us talk of other things.'

Though Sir Kenrick proposed a change of conversation he was curiously silent and absent for the next half-hour, and gave Cyril ample leisure for thought. The two young men sat smoking and looking at the fire as they had done on many a previous evening, each wrapped in his own thoughts. When the clock in the hall struck ten, Sir Kenrick emptied the ashes out of his pipe, and put it back in its proper place on the mantelpiece.

'Well, good night, old fellow,' he said, in his usual careless style. 'How soon do you think of leaving this place?'

'Before the end of the week.'

'That's sudden.'

'Yes; but you remember what the Giaour said,—

'"Better to sink beneath the shock
Than moulder piecemeal on the rock."'

Painful partings cannot be too sudden.'

'You will inconvenience Mr. Dulcimer.'

'Not much. He got on without a curate for six months before I came.'

'Where are you going?'

'To Bridford.'

'A horrible manufacturing hole!' exclaimed Sir Kenrick.

'A place where there is good work to be done by any man strong enough to do it.'

'Oh, you are mad, Cyril, that is all—a fanatic. No fakir with shrivelled arms was ever worse. But I wish you well, dear fellow, wherever you go.'

Kenrick went away, wondering at his cousin's foolishness. He did not know how far things had gone between Cyril and Beatrix, or he might have wondered still more. He thought Cyril might have won Miss Harefield by trying. He did not know she was already won.

CHAPTER IX.

'THOSE ARE THE KILLING GRIEFS WHICH DARE NOT SPEAK.'

BY slow degrees Beatrix arrived at an understanding of her position. People in Little Yafford believed her guilty of her father's murder. The idea was horrible, and she would have fled, but pride came to her rescue, and she stayed, defying all the slanderous tongues and cold cruel eyes in the village, from the judicial discourse and pale gray orbs of Miss Coyle, to the lively comments and little red-brown rat-like optics of Mr. Tudway. She met cold looks and averted heads at the church door, where she had been wont to find herself saluted with nods and becks, and a world of sympathy and friendliness. Now and then she encountered a startling glance, as of wonder that she should dare to enter the church. Even Mrs. Dulcimer was cold, and seemed embarrassed by

Beatrix's presence, though affecting all the old
cordiality. But the Vicar was full of kindness,
and tried to make up for everybody else's cruelty
His charity was not of the officious kind which
forces itself upon people who do not want it, but
it was that stronger and wider charity which is
inexhaustible for those who do. He had let
Beatrix come and go as she pleased hitherto, and
had never pressed her to remain. Now he took
her under his wing, brought her from the Water
House to the Vicarage on his arm, and let the
whole village see that he was not ashamed of
his ward.

'Mr. Dulcimer always cared too much for the
fleshpots of Egypt,' said Mrs. Coyle. 'Miss
Harefield's money blinds him to her character.
A sad thing to see a minister of the gospel so
devoted to worldly things.'

One day, stung by the disapproving look of a
face that passed her in the village street, Beatrix
made a sudden appeal to Miss Scales.

'What does it all mean?' she asked, in an
agitated voice. 'Why do these people give me

such horrible looks—or pretend not to see me? I don't want their friendship. They are nothing in the world to me. But I can't endure to live in an atmosphere of dislike. What does it mean?'

'My dear Beatrix, I had rather you did not ask me,' Miss Scales answered, stiffly.

Her manner had been gaining stiffness ever since her return from Devonshire. A deeply bordered letter had come to announce the aunt's death, and a week after there had come another letter in a blue envelope, from a local solicitor who had drawn the old lady's will, to inform Miss Scales that her aunt had appointed her sole executrix and residuary legatee. There was a legacy to the faithful old servant—a little sum in consols to provide for puss and pug—ancient favourites who had quarrelled daily for the last fifteen years—and all the rest went to Miss Scales. She was now a lady of property like her pupil, with an unencumbered estate of nearly two hundred a year.

'It would have been quite two hundred,' said

Miss Scales, 'if it hadn't been for the money in consols left to Martha. I think my aunt might have left me to provide for Martha and Floss and Fido. I should' have taken care they never wanted anything.'

'Perhaps they would rather be able to take care of themselves,' Beatrix had replied, a speech which was not agreeable to Miss Scales.

'But I must ask you,' said Beatrix, as she drove her pony carriage up the moorland road. 'Whom else can I ask? Have I so many friends ready to give me information? You must answer me.'

'I do not recognise any obligation to do so unless I choose, Beatrix,' Miss Scales replied, severely. 'The question you put is a very painful one. I cannot deny that there is an unpleasant feeling about you in people's minds. Your purchasing laudanum at different shops—forgive me if I say in an underhand and crafty manner——'

'They would not have given me enough at one shop,' interrupted Beatrix, 'and I was almost mad for want of sleep.'

'My dear, I am not finding fault with you. God

forbid that I should judge you. But, altogether, the circumstance was most unfortunate, and it has had a painful effect upon people's minds. I am not sure, Beatrix, that it would not be well for you to leave Little Yafford.'

' What ! run away from these people because they are cruel enough to believe this hideous thing ? ' cried Beatrix, passionately. ' No, that is a thing I will never do. I will live here till my hair is gray, rather than let them think their false judgment has driven me away.'

' Well, Beatrix, I am very sorry,' said Miss Scales. ' I think a tour in Switzerland—or a residence in Hanover—where you might acquire the German language with the best accent—would be good for you in every way. And, perhaps, before you came back something would transpire to convince. people they had misjudged you. However, you must do as you please, of course. I have no authority. Mr. Dulcimer is your guardian. So long as he is satisfied I cannot complain. And now, my dear, with regard to myself, I have been wishing to mention it for some time, but I did not like to say anything while your papa's death was so recent. I am going to leave you, and settle in Devonshire.'

Beatrix was petrified. She had considered Miss Scales as much a fixture as the old eight-day clock in the hall—nay, as the Water House itself, or as the massive old bridge with its single arch, which had spanned the river ever since the time of the Romans. Miss Scales was tiresome, and given to much preaching, and to the use of Johnsonian locutions, without the correctness of Johnson. She easily degenerated into a nuisance, but Beatrix was used to her, and regarded her as a part of life. Such fondness as grows out of time and custom, Beatrix had for Miss Scales, though not the affection that springs from merit and sweetness in the object of it. That Miss Scales could wish to remove herself permanently from the Water House was of all things most startling. It was as if the cedar on the lawn had uprooted itself and walked away to shade some other garden.

'Leave me!' cried Beatrix, pale with surprise. 'You can't really mean it.'

'Indeed, my dear, I do. My dearest aunt

Judson has left me a nice little independence—and at my age you would hardly expect a person to go on working.'

'There need be no work,' said Beatrix, eagerly. 'I need not trouble you any more with my studies. I can read to myself instead of to you. It will make no difference. You can have all your mornings free.'

'You cannot suppose that, so long as I remained with you, I could neglect the improvement of your mind, Beatrix,' severely exclaimed Miss Scales, fully believing in her own style of grinding—quite forty years behind the spirit of the age—as an improving process. 'No, my dear, that is not the consideration. I want to live in my own house. Dear aunt Judson has left me a *bijou* cottage at Exmouth, and all her beautiful furniture, and I feel it a duty I owe to myself, after all these years of scholastic toil, to settle down. I shall be on the spot to see after Floss and Fido, whom I should not like to leave to the care of a hireling, however well provided for.'

This was a stray javelin flung at the faithful servant, to whom Mrs. Judson had left five hundred pounds in consols.

'Oh, very well, Miss Scales, if you like Floss and Fido better than me,' said Beatrix, proudly, giving the reins a little shake that sent Puck into a canter.

'Beatrix, are you trying to murder me?' cried the terrified Miss Scales. 'Stop that pony this instant, or I'll take the reins out of your hands.'

'If you do that we shall certainly be in the ditch. There, Puck is quiet enough now.'

'As to my liking Floss and Fido better than you,' pursued Miss Scales with her judicial air, when Puck had resumed his accustomed trot, 'that is a very unfair way of putting it. I have my own happiness to consider.'

'Yes,' said Beatrix, 'that seems the first consideration with everybody.'

'If we cannot discuss this question without temper, Beatrix——' remonstrated Miss Scales.

'We cannot. At least, I cannot,' answered Beatrix, quickly. 'You have lived with me ever since I can remember. Yes, one of the first things I can remember is standing at your knee on a hot summer morning droning over a selection of the psalms, in words of one syllable. That psalm about the wicked

man and a green bay tree, for instance. I never see
a bay tree without remembering how hard it was to
learn to read. You have lived with me ever since I
was in my cradle, and yet you talk of leaving me as
coolly as if it were nothing to you.'

'My dear Beatrix, the parting will be very painful to me; but it would be more painful to remain.'

'Why?' asked Beatrix, fiercely.

'Because I could not bear to see people look
coldly upon you. I could not live in a house under
such a cloud as that which overshadows your
house.'

'I see,' cried Beatrix, her face hardening. 'You
believe what these people believe.'

'I have not said that.'

'No, you would not dare to say it. But you are
wicked enough to think it—you who have known me
all my life. This ends everything between us.'

'I should think so,' said Miss Scales. 'I shall
pack my trunks to-night, and leave Little Yafford the
first thing to-morrow morning.'

'It will be best so,' replied Beatrix, and she
turned Puck with a suddenness that swung the chaise

round in a manner to make Miss Scales a second time in fear of her life.

Beatrix drove home in silence, went straight to her own room, and shut herself in there. Her own maid, Mary, carried her up some tea, and she sent a message to Miss Scales excusing herself from going down to dinner on the ground of a headache. Had she said a heartache it would have been the truth.

Miss Scales eat her dinner in sullen state, meditating her life of independence with Floss and Fido. She asked Peacock to order a fly for her at a quarter past seven next morning, in time to catch the quarter-past eight London train at Great Yafford. She devoted the evening to packing her trunks, weeding out a few scarecrow odds and ends of finery from the garden of her wardrobe as a parting bequest to Mary. She left the Water House in the early winter gray, without having seen Beatrix. Peacock handed her an envelope at the last moment, which she opened presently in the fly. It contained no word of farewell, only bank-notes for the current quarter's salary.

This was the first absolute desertion. Beatrix

felt it heavily. She had been wounded at Bella Scratchell's keeping aloof from her, as she had done since her visit ended. She was more deeply wounded by Miss Scales's abandonment.

Before the day was out she was to receive another and much heavier blow. A letter was brought her, late in the evening, from Cyril Culverhouse. It was only the second letter she had ever received from him, but she could have sworn to his handwriting if it had been shown her among a thousand. There is no expert keener-eyed in these things than love.

'At last!' she said to herself, with a great wave of joy drowning her heart.

That the letter might bring evil tidings never occurred to her. It was like the leaflet in the beak of the dove. It meant that the dark days were ended, and the glad world was beginning to smile upon her again. The letter was long, but she had not read many lines before despair seized her. She uttered no cry or groan. She sat with the letter held tightly in her convulsed hand, devouring. the cruel words.

'MY DEAREST AND ONLY BELOVED,—Before
leaving this place I write to explain my conduct
of the last six weeks, which must have seemed
cold and unworthy, and to explain my course in the
future, which may offend her for whom I would sacrifice most things rather than offend. I have made
up my mind to leave Little Yafford. I have made
up my mind never to marry. Reasons which I
cannot enter upon have urged me to this resolution.
I have loved you deeply, fondly, with an unmeasured and absorbing love, but I have schooled
myself to surrender the hope of a happiness which
made life very fair and sweet, and which I once
deemed not incompatible with my calling and the
duties that belong to it.

' Forgive me, Beatrix, for the pain this letter may
cause you—forgive me for the part I have had in
your life. Had Providence willed for me to find you
unshackled and poor we might have been happy. As
it is, I am assured that only misery, remorse, and
regret would follow our union.

'May God bless you. May He pardon and pity
you, in all your need of pardon and pity. The best

of us need both at His hands. I take up my pilgrim's staff, with a heavy heart, and go my way, cheered by no promise in the future, sustained only by the hope of doing some good work among my fellow-men before I die.

'Oh, Beatrix, if you could know how my heart yearns towards you—how my whole being is rent as I write this cold farewell—you would pity me as I pity you—for I have need of all your pity.

'I will write no more. Words are no balm for a real and lasting sorrow.

'Farewell, Beatrix, and whatever you may think of me, believe at least that you are the only woman I have ever loved—the only woman I can ever love.

'Yours in deepest sorrow,

'CYRIL CULVERHOUSE.'

This ended all. It was very clear to her that her lover thought as Little Yafford thought. In his eyes too she was a guilty wretch, for whom he could feel nothing but pity.

'He was the only creature who ever really loved me since my mother died,' she thought, 'and now he has deserted me.'

CHAPTER X.

BELLA SCRATCHELL, tripping to the Park one frosty morning, and entering Mrs. Piper's sitting-room, all beaming with smiles, like a small edition of Aurora, found the invalid in tears, and sniffing feebly at a bottle of aromatic vinegar.

'Dear Mrs. Piper, have you had one of your bad headaches ?'

'No, my dear, it is not my bodily health, but my spiritual condition that affects me. I feel as if I had been holding on by an anchor, and somebody had taken the anchor away and left me tossing on a stormy sea. I had such faith in him. He put things in a clearer light than Mr. Mowler. The Reverend Josiah Mowler is a sainted creature—and I shall always say so, but he is not equal to Mr. Culverhouse. He hasn't the inspiration. Oh, Bella, I am grateful to you for having brought that good man here, but I feel it hard to lose him, just as I had pinned my faith upon his teaching.'

Mrs. Piper wiped away her tears with the fine hem-stitched cambric that befitted her wealth and position, and applied herself disconsolately to her smelling-bottle.

'What do you mean?' asked Bella, all the pinkness fading out of her cheeks.

'Why, surely you have heard?'

'I have heard nothing. Is it about Mr. Culverhouse?'

'My dear, he has left us. He has gone to Bridford—a horrible place in Lancashire, where they have small-pox every year. You might have knocked me down with a feather when Ebenezer came in and told me about it.'

Bella sat pale and speechless. Was it for this that she had schemed? She had slandered her familiar friend, sold herself to Satan, in the hope of winning this man; and behold! he was gone, and there was no more chance of winning him than there had been before she perilled her soul by this sin. For Bella knew that she had sinned.

She was quite capable of doing a wicked thing for her own advantage, or to gratify her evil temper, but she knew that the act was wicked, and she had a lurking idea that she would have to pay for it in some manner in the future. Bella regarded sin as some people regard going into debt for present gratification; a matter to be settled in a remote future, and hardly worth thinking about while the day of reckoning is so far off.

'Do you mean that he has really gone,' she faltered presently, 'for ever?'

'Yes, my dear, he has left us for a permanency. I suppose it is to better himself; but I can't fancy anybody bettering themselves at Bridford, where the small-pox has been raging, on and off, ever since I can remember, and where they have cholera worse than anywhere in the kingdom.'

'How did you hear of it?' asked Bella, with the faint hope that this piece of information might prove a fable.

'From himself, dear. He wrote me the sweetest

letter, full of comfort. But I don't know what I shall do without him. His visits buoyed me up.'

'Other people will be sorry,' said Bella, faintly.

'Everybody must be sorry. He is a saintly young man.'

'When did he leave?'

'Yesterday morning.'

'And I never heard of it,' exclaimed Bella.

She was thinking how all things had looked the same, though he was gone. There had been nothing in earth or sky to tell her that the light had faded out of her life. The dull village street—with her mother's vagabond fowls pecking in the highway— had looked not a shade duller than usual. She had passed Mrs. Pomfret's trim garden, and had looked tenderly at the square unpretending cottage, thinking that those walls sheltered him; and he was far away. He was gone, and she had not known it.

'He might have called to wish me good-bye,' she complained, 'after my working for his poor.'

'It must have been very sudden at the last,' suggested Mrs. Piper.

Bella went to the schoolroom to grapple with the

unruly young Pipers, sick at heart. All her misery was Mrs. Dulcimer's fault, she thought, not taking into consideration her own readiness to lend herself to Mrs. Dulcimer's plans.

There was only one ray of comfort, a lurid and unholy light, in the dark gulf of her thoughts. If Cyril had gone away taking her hopes with him, he had left Beatrix also hopeless. There was an end of the tie between those two. If he had meant to marry Miss Harefield he would not have left Little Yafford.

She dragged herself through the lesson, somehow, beating time to Elizabeth Fry's performance of the classic melody of Trab, Trab, with somebody's variations—the variations of an ancient and stereotyped order, first triplets, then little stunted runs, then octaves, then a dismal minor, all in chords, and then a general banging and flare-up for a finale. The piece was hideous, and Elizabeth Fry's playing was a degree worse than the piece. Bella's head ached woefully by the time her pupil had pounded through the brilliant finale, but she bore up heroically, and heard Horne Tooke read about William the Conqueror in a drawling voice—with a nasal *ad libitum* accompaniment. These children never seemed to get beyond William the Conqueror and his immediate posterity. Their historical ideas were strictly feudal, and it must have appeared to them only yesterday when the curfew was heard from every church tower, and Peter the Hermit was kindling the souls of Christians with his war-cry of *Deus vult*.

Bella stopped to see the little Pipers safely through their early dinner, the table of these juveniles being as much a scene of strife and contention as any battle-field in history. It was a hard matter to preserve some semblance of peace, still harder to inculcate anything approaching good manners, the young Pipers having entered the world with an incapacity for using spoons, forks, knives, or other implements of civilized life in a decent manner. The battle-field was generally flooded before dinner was over—not with the gore of the combatants, but with Brougham's stout, or with Elizabeth's regulation glass of old port, or a sauce boat that had capsized in a struggle to get it 'first,' or a mustard-pot turned over in a free fight. Bella had a little more influence over these barbarians than the servants, who, coming and going like the wind, were of no authority; but to-day Bella sat at the head of the table looking straight before her, and allowed the young Pipers to squabble, snatch, push, and kick one another to their heart's content.

She was thinking of that ideal vicarage which might have been hers in the future if Cyril Culverhouse had only cared for her.

'He might have chosen me if his heart had been free,' she reflected. 'Everybody tells me I am pretty; even Mr. Piper, coarse and common as he is, always compliments me about my looks. Why should not Cyril have liked me?'

It seemed a hard thing to Bella that this gift of prettiness should be such a barren boon, that it should not bring her exactly what she wanted. She shed some sullen tears on her way home across the windy Park, along the bleak high road. There was no one to see her tears or to pity her. She was angry with fate, angry with life, in which all things were so unequally meted out. Beatrix was miserable too, no doubt, in her handsome house yonder, the

house whose dulness Bella had found a shade worse
than poverty.

Bella changed her dress and bonnet, and went to
make an afternoon call upon Mrs. Dulcimer, certain
of hearing all about Cyril's departure from that
loquacious lady. The twilight shadows were falling
already, and the half-dozen dingy little shops in the
village street were dimly illuminated with oil or
tallow, but an hour or so before tea was always the
best time for finding Mrs. Dulcimer.

'Well, my dear, you have heard the news, I
suppose?' said the Vicar's wife, dispensing with the
usual 'how do d'ye do,' in her eagerness.

'I have, dear Mrs. Dulcimer, and I am so
surprised.'

'So is everybody, my dear, Mr. Dulcimer most of
all. Such a sudden desertion—an old pupil too, whom
we looked upon almost as a son. I think it positively
unkind. He wants a wider sphere for his work.
Such nonsense. Little Yafford has been wide
enough for Mr. Dulcimer for the last twenty years'
But the young men of the present day are so restless
and ambitious. I suppose he thinks Little Yafford

is not the shortest way to a bishopric. And he has
taken a charge at Bridford—a horrible town in
Lancashire, where there are nothing but chemical
works, and where the river runs sulphur and asafœtida.'

'Rather a perverted taste,' said Bella. 'I
wonder he did not stay here and try to marry
Miss Harefield. She would be a splendid match
for him. And now her father is dead she is free
to marry any one she likes.'

Mrs. Dulcimer shook her head with a dismal
air, and gave a prolonged sigh.

'Ah, my dear, it is very sad. Those reports!'
Bella echoed the sigh.

'I was very fond of her—once,' she said.

'So was I, Bella. And, even now, I should
be the last to condemn her. God forbid that
I should judge anybody. I hope I know the
gospel too well for that. But I confess that I
cannot feel the same as I used about Beatrix
Harefield. I can't get over the strangeness of
her having bought that laudanum in ever so
many different shops. There 'seems such a low

cunning in it—it is like the act of a criminal,' continued Mrs. Dulcimer, warming as she went on, and forgetting her protest against judging others. 'And I am sorry to say,' she continued, with increasing solemnity, 'Rebecca thinks as I do.'

'And Mr. Dulcimer?' inquired Bella.

'Oh, Mr. Dulcimer is a very curious man in that respect. He never thinks the same as other people. He is convinced of Beatrix's innocence, and says the Little Yafford people are a set of venomous idiots for condemning her. But say what he will, he cannot stem the tide of public opinion. The coroner's verdict was so unsatisfactory.'

'What does Sir Kenrick think?' asked Bella.

'Oh, he and Mr. Dulcimer are of the same opinion.'

'Beatrix is too handsome to be condemned by gentlemen,' said Bella, with unconscious venom.

'Oh, my dear, that consideration would not affect Mr. Dulcimer, however it might influence Kenrick. The best thing she could do would be to marry Kenrick,' pursued Mrs. Dulcimer, thought-

fully, 'but I could never take the same interest
in the match that I should have done a few
months ago. In fact, I would rather not have
act or part in it. If they were to marry, and
Kenrick were to die suddenly—or under mysterious circumstances, and I had been the means
of bringing about the marriage, I should feel
myself a murderer.'

Mr. Dulcimer came in from his afternoon
round at this moment. He nodded to Bella, and
sank down with a fatigued air in the comfortable
arm-chair that always stood ready for him in the
snuggest corner of the hearth.

'I have been to the Water House,' he said,
as if taking up the thread of his wife's discourse.
'Beatrix is very ill.'

'I am sorry to hear that.'

'I am more than sorry. These wretches will
contrive to kill her before they have done. Namby
says that her illness is entirely the result of mental
disturbance. That monster Scales has gone off at a
moment's notice—after eating Harefield's bread for
fifteen years—and left that poor child to face this

foul-mouthed world alone. She is ill—and with no one but servants about her. You ought to go and nurse her, Bella. She has been very good to you. I hope you are not a fair-weather friend, like the old man in the weather-glass, who only comes out when the sun is shining.'

'Oh, Mr. Dulcimer, how can you think so badly of me?' remonstrated Bella.

'I don't wish to think badly about you. But you have rather deserted Beatrix lately, I have noticed.'

'Mrs. Piper is so exacting, and such an invalid.'

'Well, Beatrix is also an invalid now, and Mrs. Piper must give way a little. She has her husband and children to take care of her. Beatrix has no one. As soon as she is well enough to be moved I shall have her brought here.'

'Oh, Clement!' exclaimed Mrs. Dulcimer, with a troubled look.

'What do you mean by "Oh, Clement"? We have plenty of spare bedrooms. Providence, in denying us children, has balanced matters by giving us spare bedrooms.'

'Don't you think people will talk if we have her here?'

'People will talk whether or no. The business in life of one half of the world is to criticise and misjudge the conduct of the other half. But have you ever reflected how little difference all this evil speaking makes in life? It cannot change a single element in nature. It can worry us into untimely graves, if we are foolish enough to be worried by it— it can divide man and wife, or father and son, if man or wife, or father or son, is idiotic enough to be influenced by the evil tongues of indifferent lookers on—but scandal cannot, of itself, make the slightest difference in us or in the world we inhabit. It cannot shorten our days or prevent the summer sun from shining upon us.'

'I am sure I don't know what Miss Coyle will say,' murmured Mrs. Dulcimer, plaintively.

'Miss Coyle is not my bishop,' retorted her husband, 'and if she were I should not consult her as to my choice of guests.'

Bella went to the Water House next day. She found Beatrix prostrate with some kind of low fever,

and light-headed. It was altogether a piteous spec-
tacle, this lonely sick bed. Mr. Namby came in
three times in the course of the day and evening,
and was full of anxiety about his patient. He found
Bella sitting quietly by the bedside, ready to assist
the faithful maid-servant in nursing her mistress.
Mrs. Peters, the fat housekeeper, came in every half-
hour, and was miserable because her beef tea and
calves' foot jelly were not appreciated by the fever-
parched invalid.

Cyril's name came more than once from those
dry pale lips, while Bella sat by and listened. His
desertion was evidently the blow that had struck
home.

'I'm afraid she's heard some of the unkind gossip
that's been about, and that it has preyed upon her
mind,' said Mr. Namby, in a confidential chat with
Miss Scratchell. 'I can't account for her illness in
any other way. It's all the mind. Mr. Dulcimer
promises to carry her off to the Vicarage directly she
is well enough to be moved. That will be a very
good thing. Change—change of scene and surroundings will do a great deal.'

To Mr. Namby, whose horizon had for the last
five-and-thirty years been bounded by the sulky
ridge of the moor that shut in Little Yafford, a
change from the Water House to the Vicarage
seemed a grand thing. And if in the summer his
patient could be taken to Scarborough or Harrogate,
the cure ought to be complete. Mr. Namby never
thought of prescribing the Tyrol or the Engadine.
Those places had for him little more than a tradi-
tionary or geographical existence, and were only
present in his mind as certain wavy lines upon the
map. The days of Cook and Gaze, when even such
persons as Mr. Namby may be personally conducted
over the face of the Continent, were yet to come.

Beatrix mended slowly under Mr. Namby's care,
and with plenty of nursing from Mrs. Peters, Mary
the housemaid, Bella, and Mrs. Dulcimer; the Vicar's
wife being incapable of remaining long in a state of
even tacit opposition to her dear Clement. She was
not quite comfortable in her own mind about Beatrix,
but she tried to be convinced, and she told herself
that such a clever man as Clement, whose opinions
were supported by the finest library of reference that

ever a country parson collected, must be wiser than Miss Coyle.

So one afternoon in windy March, Beatrix was put into the old-fashioned carriage in which her mother had driven during her brief wedded life, and was conveyed to the Vicarage, there to remain till she should be strong enough to travel. She felt a sensation nearer akin to happiness than she had known for a long time when she found herself seated in the Vicar's firelit library, with a little old-fashioned tea-table by her side, and Rebecca waiting upon her with a cup of strong tea. Rebecca had been talked to seriously by the Vicar, and had seceded in a scandalously abrupt manner from the Coyle faction.

'Now, Beatrix, this is to be your home as long as you can make yourself happy in it,' said the Vicar. 'The Water House is a very fine old place, but it is damp and dismal, and I don't at all wonder that it made you ill. You are to call this home, and you are to think of me as your father.'

'And you do not believe——' faltered Beatrix, and then burst into tears.

'I believe you are a good and noble girl,' said

the Vicar, cheerily, 'and that a happy and honourable life lies before you.'

'And after all,' he reflected, 'though I detest match-making, it would be no bad thing for that dog Kenrick if he could win this splendid girl for his wife.'

That dog Kenrick was still staying, off and on, at the Vicarage. His leave did not expire till the end of April. He had about six weeks before him.

He came in presently while Beatrix was sitting in the dimly lighted room sipping her tea. Mr. Dulcimer had been called out into the hall to see a parishioner. There was no one else in the room.

'I am so glad to see you better,' said Kenrick, heartily, planting himself in a chair near Miss Harefield.

By that doubtful light he was wonderfully like Cyril. The shock of his entrance—something in the likeness, as he sat beside her with the fire-glow flickering upon his face, moved Beatrix painfully. She could hardly answer him.

'Thank you. I am much better,' she murmured, faintly.

'But far from well, I am afraid,' he said. 'You seem very weak.'

In the next instant her head fell back upon the cushion of the easy chair. She had fainted. Kenrick rang the bell violently for Rebecca.

He was not a coxcomb, but he had a very good opinion of himself, and this fainting fit of Beatrix's affected himself curiously. He made up his mind that it was he whom she loved, and not Cyril; and he made up his mind that he would win her for his wife.

CHAPTER XI.

SLOWLY and gradually health and strength came back to Beatrix Harefield. The family life at the Vicarage was a new thing to her. It was a new thing to live in a house where everybody was cheerful, and where people seemed fond of her. The library was her favourite room, and Mr. Dulcimer her chosen companion. Whether he was silently absorbed in his book, or laid it down, as he did very often, to talk to her, Beatrix found his society all-sufficient. She read and studied at a table he had allotted to her, apart from him, and yet near him. Under his guidance she read the books that filled her mind with the best material; she climbed from height to height upon the hills of knowledge. New worlds opened to her that she had never dreamed of, and she went in and found that there were pleasant regions in those strange worlds. Science, which she had only known as a name, opened its treasure-house for her. Art, which she had known almost as vaguely, was revealed to her, with all its mysteries and beauties, unknown to the ignorant. And Poetry, best and sweetest of all, in her mind, opened the door to a fairy-land of inexhaustible delight. She did not forget Cyril, but she learned to look with a calm disdain upon her maligners in Little Yafford, and she was almost happy.

Before the end of March Mrs. Dulcimer had broken altogether with Miss Coyle, after rebuking that ancient sibyl, in no measured phrase, for her want of charity.

'I shall never drop in to tea here again,' said Mrs. Dulcimer. 'No, Miss Coyle, not if we both were to live for a hundred years.'

'I shall be very sorry for that,' replied Miss Coyle, sitting very erect behind her oval tea-tray, and with her gaze fixed upon her silver teapot, marked with King George's pigtail, and an heir-loom; 'but I cannot alter my opinion, even,' with a tremulous movement of her cannon curls, 'for the privilege of retaining Mrs. Dulcimer's friendship. I can only say, and I shall say so while the power of speech is left me, that Miss Harefield is a young person I would never consent to receive in my house — no, not if her thousands were millions.'

'Fortunately Miss Harefield does not want to come into your house,' retorted Mrs. Dulcimer, very red and angry, and with all her frillings and puffings in agitation. 'Thousands, indeed! Do you suppose Beatrix Harefield's fortune has any influence with Mr. Dulcimer or me?'

'I don't presume to speculate upon Mr. Dulcimer's motives or yours, but I believe the coroner's jury would have come to a very different verdict if Miss Harefield had been poor and a stranger. Look at the men who were on the jury. Why, there was Haslope the grocer, who has served the Water House ever since he has been in trade; and Ridswell the upholsterer, who had the order for the funeral. Slavish creatures who have fattened upon the Harefield family! Of course they would not condemn the daughter of their patron.'

'What proof can you bring against her ?'

'Enough to hang her if she had been anybody else,' said Miss Coyle. 'Why did she buy that laudanum ?'

'For her own use.'

'Ah!' said Miss Coyle.

There is a great deal of meaning in the monosyllable 'Ah!' if it be uttered with a grave shake of the head, a tightening of thin lips, and a prolongation of tone.

'I don't think there is any Christian feeling in Little Yafford,' exclaimed Mrs. Dulcimer, drawing on a tight glove, and bursting it in a ruinous manner.

'Except at the Vicarage,' sneered Miss Coyle

'The place is given over to a pack of prying old maids and spiteful old bachelors.'

'Thank you,' said Miss Coyle, with withering sarcasm.'

She rose to accompany Mrs. Dulcimer to the door. She was not going to fail in politeness, even to a departing foe.

'Good afternoon, and good-bye,' said the Vicar's wife, walking along the little garden path with an air of shaking the dust of Miss Coyle's tenement from off her shoes.

From this time forward Mrs. Dulcimer took Beatrix under her wing. She forgot that she too had shared the dark suspicions of Little Yafford. It was in her mind as if those suspicions had never been. She was a woman who lived from hand to mouth. Her ideas were the ideas of to-day; yesterday's convictions went for nothing. She told Rebecca that she was disgusted with the people of Little Yafford for their infamous conduct to Beatrix; and Rebecca, who, though of too sterling metal to be a time-server, loved to please her mistress, went over to Miss Harefield's party, and defended her stoutly at all kitchen tea parties.

And Sir Kenrick—Sir Kenrick, who had always despised her slanderers, was now Beatrix Harefield's most ardent champion. He had begun by thinking that she would make an admirable mistress of Culverhouse Castle; he ended by being very sure that she would make an adorable wife. He left off fishing for sulky pike in the reedy pools and inlets of the winding river, and spent his days hanging about the Vicarage, idle and happy, and very much in the way of other people's industry. The lynx eyes of Mrs. Dulcimer, trained to see very far into all budding loves, were quick to perceive the state of affairs. She was delighted, and forgot that she had ever abandoned her plans for the union of the impoverished Culverhouse estate, and the fat fields and rich pastures of the Harefield property. It seemed to her the realization of her own idea. She took Kenrick's young affection under her protection; she smiled fondly upon the unconscious Beatrix. She was full of Machiavellian schemes for leaving the two young people in each other's society. The end of Kenrick's leave was drawing near. Things were getting desperate, Mrs. Dulcimer thought. It must be now or never. She even went so far as to tell Kenrick so.

'Faint heart never won fair lady,' she said. 'I know she likes you.'

'I hope you won't think me conceited if I agree with you, but I really think she does,' said Kenrick, remembering that curious fainting fit on the first evening of Miss Harefield's visit.

He took heart of grace next day, finding Beatrix alone in the library an hour or so before the late tea. It was a windy afternoon, late in March, the sky dull and gray, the wood fire glowing redly, Beatrix seated in her low chair beside the hearth, with a book on her lap, deep in thought.

'I don't wonder you admire Pascal,' she said, without looking up, as Kenrick came towards the hearth. 'His is a most delicate wit.'

'I am sorry to say I don't know anything about the gentleman,' said Kenrick. 'Did he write plays or novels?'

'I beg your pardon. I thought you were Mr. Dulcimer.'

'You took me for a better man than I am. All those rows of sober old books are Greek to me—worse than Greek, for I do know that by sight. I wonder that you can find so much happiness in this dry-as-dust collection of the dear Vicar's.'

'I don't know about happiness,' answered Beatrix, with a faint sigh. 'I find forgetfulness. I suppose that is almost as good.'

'There cannot be much in your young life that you can wish to forget,' said Kenrick.

'There is very little in it that I care to remember.'

'Erase it altogether from your memory then, and begin a new life from to-day," said Kenrick, flinging himself head foremost into a gulf of uncertain issues, like the diver who plunges into the fatal deep to win the king's daughter. 'Let the beginning of a brighter and happier life date from to-day. You are one of those flowers of earth which seem to be born to blush unseen. You, who are so worthy of love and admiration, have lived hidden from those who could admire and appreciate. But if a real and unmeasured love in the present can compensate for your losses in the past, that love is yours, Beatrix. I love you as I never thought I should love. I did not know that it was in my nature to feel as strongly as I feel for you. Stop—do not answer me too quickly,' he cried, reading rejection in her look as she turned to him with the firelight shining on her face. 'You will say, perhaps, "I am rich and you are poor. How am I to believe in your truth?"'

'I am not capable of thinking meanly of you,' answered Beatrix. 'But you ask me what is impossible. I have made up my mind never to marry.'

'Will you tell me the reason?'

'That is my secret.'

'I am not to be answered so easily, Beatrix. I love you too well to lose you without a struggle. I have spoken too soon, perhaps. I have been too precipitate. But I am to go back to India in a few weeks, and I should like to return with a new happiness—with at least the promise of your love.'

'I have no love to give you. If you could see into the bottom of my heart, you would be horrified at its emptiness. The warmest feeling I have is gratitude to my friends the Dulcimers. Yes, I think that is the only human feeling you would discover in my heart. That is why I like to live among these books. They are a world in themselves. They give me delight, and ask no love in return.'

'But I am not like the books, Beatrix; I ask for your love, and I shall not be easily denied.'

And then he told her his dream about Culverhouse Castle. How she was to reign there—not like his mother, in silence and seclusion, but in all the power of youth, beauty, and wealth, a queen of county society, the centre and focus of a happy world of her own, loved, admired, and revered.

'I,' exclaimed Beatrix—'I, who have been suspected of poisoning my father?'

'That shameful slander has never penetrated beyond this contemptible hole,' said Kenrick, very disrespectful to Little Yafford in the warmth of his indignation. 'For God's sake, Beatrix, do not let that foul scandal weigh in your mind. Perhaps that is the reason you reject me,' he added, slow to believe that he had been mistaken when he fancied himself beloved.

'No,' answered Beatrix, 'but the only man I ever loved rejected me for that reason.'

'Oh,' said Kenrick, deeply mortified.

After this confession he could no longer doubt that he had mistaken Beatrix's feelings towards him. He was silent for some minutes, and then he exclaimed suddenly,—

'That man was my cousin Cyril?'

'He was.'

'Then my cousin Cyril is a mean hound.'

'Do you want me to hate you?' cried Beatrix, angrily. 'He is not mean. He is all that is good and noble. Why should his pure life be sullied by the taint that has fallen upon mine? He, a clergyman, could not afford to take a wife whom men have suspected of evil. He is like Cæsar. His wife must be above suspicion. He loved me once. He will love me always, perhaps, a little better than all other women, as I shall love him to the end of life above all other men. But he has chosen something better in this life than a woman's love. He has given himself to the service of God. No unholy thing must come within the veil of the temple. Nothing stained, not even with the suspicion of sin, must enter there. A priest's wife must be spotless.'

'If he could suspect you,' exclaimed Kenrick, vindictively, 'he is unworthy——'

'Oh, for pity's sake do not suggest that,' interrupted Beatrix. 'I cannot believe that he could suspect me, having once known and loved me. It was not his suspicion, but the evil thoughts of others, that parted us.'

'Then he is a coward,' cried Kenrick, honestly angry. 'A man's choice of his wife is a question of life or death for himself. He is both craven and fool if he allows other people to be the arbiters of his fate.'

'But you do not understand,' urged Beatrix, pleading for the man who had broken her heart. 'It is his office——'

'His office be——'

He might have said something very shocking if Mrs. Dulcimer had not come in at this moment. She found Beatrix in tears, and Kenrick pacing up and down the room with a distracted air. These two facts indicated that something decisive had happened, and Mrs. Dulcimer saw from Kenrick's face that the something was of an unsatisfactory nature.

' How provoking !' she thought. ' It really seems as if no plan of mine is to succeed.'

Beatrix did not appear at the tea-table. She sent an apology by Rebecca. She had a headache, and would go to bed early. Kenrick was absent-minded, and out of spirits. The meal, usually so cheerful, was eaten in silence ; Mr. Dulcimer had picked up a queer little seventeenth century copy of Boileau at Great Yafford that morning, and looked at the tail-pieces and initials as he took his tea.

' Stop and smoke your cigar here, Ken,' said Mrs. Dulcimer when tea was over, and Sir Kenrick was about to follow his host to the library.

' But don't you dislike smoke in this room ? '

' Not for once in a way. Your cigars are very mild, and Rebecca will air the room well to-morrow morning. I want to have a chat with you.'

' Delighted,' said Kenrick, sitting down opposite Mrs. Dulcimer's work-table.

He had a shrewd suspicion of what was coming, but he felt that it would comfort him to pour his woes into a friendly ear. He knew very well that

Mrs. Dulcimer had set her heart upon his marrying Miss Harefield.

'What had you been doing to make Beatrix cry?' asked the Vicar's wife, coming straight to the point.

'I had asked her to be my wife.'

'What, they were tears of joy then?' cried Mrs. Dulcimer.

'Quite the contrary. She had rejected me flatly.'

'Oh, Kenrick! But why?'

'She did not condescend to enter very minutely into her reasons, but I believe the principal one is that she doesn't care for me.'

'Oh, Kenrick,' cried Mrs. Dulcimer, in exactly the same tone as before. 'What a pity!'

'Yes, it's regretable. If my first thought were her fortune and the good it would do to Culverhouse, I should deserve my fate. But that is only my second thought. I love her very dearly. If she were the poorest little nursery governess in the county I should love her just the same, and would take her back to India with me, and work for her and be happy with her all the days of my life.'

'But her money would pay off those mortgages;

as Lady Culverhouse she would have a leading position in your part of the country.'

'She would be admired and adored,' said Kenrick.

'It would be in every way such a suitable match,' protested Mrs. Dulcimer, a remark she was in the habit of making about every pair of young people whose footsteps she wished to direct to the hymeneal altar. 'Really human nature is very perverse.'

She remembered how ignominiously she had failed in her desire to benefit Cyril and Bella; and here was this more important scheme apparently doomed to failure.

'It is very difficult to serve one's fellow-creatures,' she said presently. 'But this is not a business to be given up lightly, Kenrick. This foolish girl is Mr. Dulcimer's ward, and it is his duty to see her advantageously settled in life. Now Clement is the very last man to think of such a thing. He considers he has done his duty when he has given Beatrix the run of his library.'

'Yes,' said Kenrick. 'It is dear Dulcimer's only

fault to consider books the beginning, middle, and end of life.'

'Something must be done,' declared Mrs. Dulcimer, with a sudden accession of energy. 'Beatrix ought to marry, and she ought to marry a man of position. I cannot imagine a more suitable husband than yourself. Come, Kenrick, be frank with me. You have not told me everything. There must be some other reason. Don't you remember an admission Beatrix made at that dreadful inquest? There was a love affair of which her father disapproved. Nothing but a prior attachment could prevent her accepting you. I feel convinced it must be that.'

'It is that,' answered Kenrick. 'You can keep a secret, I suppose, Mrs. Dulcimer?'

'My dear Kenrick, I have kept hundreds.'

This was true, but Mrs. Dulcimer forgot to add how short a time she had kept them. The Vicar's wife's secret of to-day was the town-crier's secret of to-morrow.

'Then I'll trust you with the clue to the mystery. There is a prior attachment—to my cousin Cyril.'

' Good heavens!' exclaimed Mrs. Dulcimer. 'Then that is why he was so indifferent to poor Bella Scratchell, the very girl for him.'

' He is a contemptible cur,' said Kenrick.

He went on to abuse his cousin roundly. It was a good thing for him, no doubt, that Cyril had behaved so badly, for it gave Kenrick just the chance that Beatrix would put the false lover out of her mind and marry the true one. He told Mrs. Dulcimer everything.

'Something must be done,' she said finally, and she made up her mind that she, Selina Dulcimer, was the right person to undertake the task.

CHAPTER XII.

SOMETHING MUST BE DONE.

BEFORE Sir Kenrick's leave came to an end Mrs. Piper had gone to the land where there are no sordid cares, no gnawing doubts as to the honesty of servants, no heart-corroding regrets at the wastefulness and expenditure of a large household. Mrs. Piper had gone to that undiscovered country where we may fairly hope that for those who have lived harmlessly upon earth all is peace. Mr. Piper drove his smart little pony cart about the country roads and through the village street as usual, but he wore an altered countenance and crape to the top of his tall hat. He no longer had a noisy greeting for every one, no longer quoted Jeremy Bentham or William Cobbett. Never was widower more disconsolate than Ebenezer Piper. Honestly and truly he mourned the careful partner of his youth and maturity.

'There wasn't a finer girl in Great Yafford when

me and she was married,' he said dolefully, after a brief eulogium of his faithful Moggie's domestic virtues.

Mrs. Piper's monument was to be the glory of the village churchyard. Mr. Dulcimer was too indulgent and easy to insist upon a rigid æstheticism in the memorials which the living erected in honour of the dead. There was a good deal of bad taste in God's Acre at Little Yafford, but Mr. Piper was destined to put the cap on the edifice by the gaudiest and most expensive mausoleum that ever the chief stonemason of Great Yafford had devised or executed.

It was to be a sarcophagus of the jewel casket shape, with four twisted columns, like candlesticks, at the corners, and a tall urn surmounting the lid. Each of the columns was of a different coloured marble, the urn was dark red serpentine, with a malachite serpent coiled round it. The urn was supposed to contain Mrs. Piper's dust, the serpent indicated that physicians and doctors' stuff had not been wanting in the effort to keep Mrs. Piper longer upon earth. Scattered over the fluted lid of the sarcophagus were to be flowers sculptured out of coloured marble, and cemented on to the white groundwork. The sides of the sarcophagus were to be decorated with shields, richly emblazoned with the Piper arms. Mr. Piper's arms were his own composition ; his crest a ladder; his motto, *Ex sese.*

Altogether the monument was to be a wonderful thing, and Mr. Piper felt a pride in contemplating the sketches which the mason had caused to be made, and in picturing to himself the effect of the whole when this great work of art should be finished.

The Piper children, in black frocks, and in a state of semi-orphanage, were a little more troublesome than they had been in coloured frocks, and with an invalid mamma as a court of appeal. They brought the ghost of their lost parent into every argument.

'I'm sure ma wouldn't have wished me to learn three verbs in one morning,' said Elizabeth Fry.

'I think ma would have let me off my lessons if I had a sick headache,' remonstrated Mary Wolstencroft.

'I shall do my duty to you whether you like it or no,' said Bella, resolutely.

'Ah, you'd better take care!' cried Brougham. 'Ma's in heaven, where she can see everything you're up to, and won't she make it disagreeable for you when you get there! If you ever do,' added the boy, in a doubtful tone; 'but I don't think you stand much chance if you go on making our lives a misery with Latin grammar.'

Now that poor Mrs. Piper had laid down her load of earthly care, Miss Scratchell restricted her visits to the Park to purely professional limits. She entered the schoolroom punctually at nine, and she left it as punctually at half-past one. She no longer assisted at the children's early dinner, a meal which Mr. Piper, when at home, shared under the name of luncheon. Bella had a keen sense of the proprieties, and did not care to sit down to luncheon with a disconsolate widower, or to give Mr. Piper any opportunity to pour his griefs into her ear, as he would fain have done very often. Mr. Piper was of a soft and affectionate nature, and when he told his griefs to a young woman he could not refrain from taking her hand, and even occasionally squeezing it. This Bella could not possibly permit. She therefore carefully avoided all conversations about the late Mrs. Piper, and, as far as was practicable, she avoided Mr. Piper himself.

'It seems very 'ard,' complained the widower, 'that the time when a man feels lonesomest is a time for everybody to avide him. You might as well stop, Miss Scratchell, and eat your bit of dinner with me and the children. You won't get lamb and sparrowgrass at home.'

'I know I shall not,' replied Bella; 'but I would rather not stay, thank you, Mr. Piper.'

'Why not?'

'My mother wants me at home.'

'She can't want you more now than she did when pore Mrs. P—— was alive. You never refused to stop then.'

'I did not like to refuse dear Mrs. Piper, when she was an invalid, and wanted every one's sympathy.'

'You're a good-'earted girl,' said Piper, approvingly. 'I know what your motive is. You think it ain't proper to eat your bit of dinner with me, now I'm a widower, though there's all the children to keep you in countenance. You think it might set the old tabbies up street talking.'

'It certainly does not require much to do that,' replied Bella, smiling. 'But I really am wanted at home, Mr. Piper, and I mustn't stop talking here. I am going to drink tea at the Vicarage this evening.'

'Ah!' sighed Mr. Piper, 'you're a rum girl. It seems to me that everybody wants you. I shall send you round a bundle of my early sparrow-grass.'

'Pray don't take the trouble.'

'Yes, I shall. It costs me about eighteen-pence a stick, so somebody may as well have the enjoyment of it. But 'orticulture is my 'obby.'

It must be observed that although Mr. Piper was a student of Cobbett, and had taught himself a little Latin, he had never been able to conquer the mysteries of his own tongue. He still spoke as bad

English as in the days when he was a factory hand, and had never read a passage of Cobbett's strong racy prose, or pondered over a thesis of Bentham's.

Bella and Beatrix were good friends still, but not such friends as they had been a year or even six months ago. There was a restraint on both sides. Beatrix could not have told why it was, but it seemed to her that there was a change in herself, and a still greater change in Bella. Bella knew very well what it was that made her uncomfortable in Miss Harefield's society. It was the sealed letter in its hiding-place in Bella's shabby old bedroom. That sealed letter weighed like a load of iron upon Bella's conscience when she found herself in Beatrix's company; and yet she was glad that she had done this thing, if it had been the means of parting Cyril and Beatrix.

She would like to have seen them parted even more irrevocably, so that under no circumstances could time or chance bring them together again. She was in this temper of mind when she went to spend the evening at the Vicarage, after her little talk with Mr. Piper in the stone portico at the Park.

It was about a week since Sir Kenrick had made his offer and had been rejected. He had taken a wonderful fancy to fishing for pike after that catastrophe, and had brought home some very handsome specimens of that ravenous tribe, for the Vicarage cook to stuff and bake, and serve with savoury sauces for the three o'clock dinner.

'I think I shall have to protest, like the highland gillies when they got too much salmon, if Kenrick goes on bringing home pike in this way,' said Mr. Dulcimer, when the cover was lifted and the hungry-jawed scaly monster appeared before him.

Kenrick was off in the early gray to his fishing grounds, so he and Beatrix only met of an evening. He was very polite to her, and evidently bore no malice. Hope was not altogether extinguished in his breast. He had much confidence in Mrs. Dulcimer, who had said that something must be done. Kenrick had not the faintest idea what this inveterate match-maker meant to do, but he felt that her friendship would stick at nothing which a clergyman's wife might do without peril to her soul.

'Bella,' said Mrs. Dulcimer after tea, 'I want to

show you the things I've made for the missionary basket. You might be able to help me a little, perhaps.'

'I shall be delighted, dear Mrs. Dulcimer,' answered Bella, inwardly lamenting that it had pleased God to call her to that station of life in which her friends always felt themselves justified in asking her to work for them.

A young woman of fortune like Miss Harefield might be as idle or as selfish as she pleased. Nobody ever thought of asking for payment in kind for any favour they showed her; but everybody who did any kindness to penniless Bella Scratchell wanted to extort recompense for his or her civility in needle-work or some sort of drudgery.

'Come up to my room and look at the things, dear,' said Mrs. Dulcimer; and then it occurred to Bella that her hostess had something particular to say to her. She had heard from Cyril that day, perhaps, or had got news of him by a side wind. Bella's heart beat ever so fast at the idea.

They went up to Mrs. Dulcimer's bedroom, a large old-fashioned chamber, with an immense four-post bedstead and flowery chintz curtains, a muslin-draped dressing-table, adorned with a great many china pots, and a pin-cushion that was a noteworthy feature. Mrs. Dulcimer's devotional books—with a great many markers in them, looking as if they were read immensely—were arranged on either side of the looking-glass. She used to read Taylor's ' Holy Living ' while Rebecca put her hair in papers of an evening. She did not read the ' Holy Dying.' It seemed a great deal too soon for that.

There was a bright fire, and the chintz-covered sofa was wheeled in front of it. Between the fire and the sofa was Mrs. Dulcimer's work-table, and on the table the missionary basket full of inge-nious trifles, useful or useless. Babies' socks, muffa-tees, pincushions of every shape and design, and a variety of the aggravating family of mats.

'Bella,' said Mrs. Dulcimer, when they were seated on the sofa, ' I have something particular to say to you.'

And then the Vicar's wife told Bella her plan for marrying Kenrick and Beatrix, and how Beatrix had refused Kenrick on account of her attachment to his cousin.

'Isn't it a pity, Bella?' she asked, after lengthily expounding all this.

'Yes,' answered Bella, looking thoughtful, 'they would have suited each other very well, I should think.'

'Think!' cried Mrs. Dulcimer. 'There's no thinking about it. They were made for each other.'

Mrs. Dulcimer's couples always were made for each other. It is odd how many of them turned out misfits.

Bella was reflecting that if Beatrix were happily married to Sir Kenrick Culverhouse, her sin about the sealed letter would weigh less heavily on her conscience—or, indeed, need not weigh at all. What can any one ask more than happiness? And, in the eye of the world, Kenrick was a much more suitable husband for a young woman of fortune than Cyril could possibly be.

'Now I have been thinking,' continued Mrs. Dulcimer, sinking to a mysterious undertone, 'that perhaps if Beatrix could be made to think that Cyril was fickle and inconstant, and that before he left Little Yafford he had got to care for some one else—you, for instance,' whispered Mrs. Dulcimer, making a little stab at Bella with her forefinger, 'it might cure her of her foolish attachment to him. It is ridiculous that she should go on caring for a man who doesn't love her, when there is a noble young fellow who does love her passionately, and can make her Lady Culverhouse. If she could only be made to think that Cyril was fond of you, Bella, without actual falsehood,' concluded Mrs. Dulcimer, with a strong emphasis upon the qualifying adjective, as much as to say that in so good a cause she would not mind sailing rather near the wind.

'I'm sure I don't know how it is to be done,' said Bella, with a meditative air. 'Beatrix is so self-opinionated. It is not as if she were a weak-minded pliable girl. She is as hard as rock.'

'But you are so clever, Bella. You could manage anything. If I were to say now that I always thought Cyril was very fond of you—and I did think so for a long time, as you know, dear —and if you were to say something that would sustain that idea. We need neither of us tell an actual story.'

'Of course not,' answered Bella, piously. 'Do

you suppose I would tell a story, dear Mrs. Dulcimer ?'

'Indeed no, my love. I know how truthful you are.'

Thus it was agreed between the Vicar's wife and her ductile *protégée* that, somehow or other, Beatrix was to be persuaded that her lover had been doubly false to her; false in abandoning her because evil tongues maligned her, false in preferring another woman.

CHAPTER XIII.

BY what serpentine twists and windings Bella Scratchell reached the end she had in view need not be recorded. She was by nature a creature of many curves, and all her progress in life was devious and indirect. Enough that she succeeded in making Beatrix Harefield believe her lost lover false and fickle, and thus undermined the girl's respect for the man who had renounced her. So long as Beatrix could believe that Cyril had sacrificed his heart's desire to his duty as priest and teacher, she would have continued to reverence and love him. Present or absent, he would have remained the one central figure in her life. From the moment she was persuaded to think him the shallow lover of a day—or indeed, worse than this, a lover who had been drawn to her by the lure of her wealth, and who at the bottom of his heart had always preferred Bella's lilies and roses—from that moment she despised him, and concentrated all the forces of her mind in the endeavour to forget him.

'I will never pray for him or his work again,' she vowed to herself, and the vow had all the savagery of a pagan oath. 'His name shall never pass my lips or find a place in my heart. It shall be to me as if such a man had never lived.'

From this time there was a marked change in her manner. It was brighter, gayer, harder than it had been before. That mournful resignation which had distinguished her since her father's death gave place to a proud indifference, a careless scorn of all things and all men, save the few friends she liked and trusted. That disgust of life which attacks most of us at odd times, and which sometimes afflicts even the young, had seized upon her. All things in this world were hateful to her. Solomon, sated with wealth and glory, could not have felt the emptiness of earthly joys more deeply than this girl of nineteen, whose lips had scarcely touched the cup of life. She knew herself rich, and with all good things at

her disposal—beautiful enough to command the love
of men ; and yet, because that one man whom she
loved had proved false and unworthy, she turned
with a sickened soul from all that earth held of hope
or pleasure.   Unhappily she had not yet learned to
look higher for comfort.   She was not irreligious.
She firmly believed all her Church taught her to
believe, but she had not learned, like Hezekiah, to
lay her trouble before the Lord.   She locked up her
grief in her own heart, as something apart from her
spiritual life; and she went on conforming outwardly
to all the duties of religion, but deriving no inward
solace from her faith.

Beatrix was in this mood when Mrs. Dulcimer,
delighted at Bella's speedy success, but opining,
nevertheless, that something more must be done,
was seized with a happy idea.

'Kenrick,' she exclaimed at tea one evening,
when Kenrick had announced his intention of going
to have one more peep at Culverhouse Castle before
he embarked on board the P. and O. steamship that
was to carry him on the first stage of his journey to
India—'Kenrick,' cried Mrs. Dulcimer, with an ex-

cited air, 'I really think it is the oddest thing in the world.'

'What, dear Mrs. Dulcimer?' asked Kenrick, while everybody else looked curious.

'Why, that after knowing you all these years, and hearing you talk so much about Culverhouse Castle, we should never have seen it.'

'I don't know whom you mean by we,' said Mr. Dulcimer, 'but I beg to say that I spent three weeks at Culverhouse in one of my long vacations, and a capital time I had there. The Avon is one of the finest salmon rivers I ever fished in.'

'Ah, that was in Kenrick's father's time,' said Mrs. Dulcimer; 'but though you may be perfectly quainted with the place, Clement, I have never seen it.'

'That is your own fault,' exclaimed Kenrick. 'Nothing would make me happier than to receive you there. It would be something in the style of the famous reception at Wolf's Crag, perhaps, especially if it were in the close time for salmon; but you should have a hearty welcome, and I shouldn't feel my position so keenly as the Master of Ravenswood felt his.'

'There would be no Lucy Ashton in the case,' put in the Vicar, innocently.

'And should we really not put you out if we came?' asked Mrs. Dulcimer.

'Not the least in the world. You would have to live as plainly as Eton boys, that is all. My housekeeper can roast a joint and boil a potato. I think she might even manage a bit of fish, and a rhubarb tart. We would not quite starve you, and I know you would be charmed with the dear old place; but if you are coming you must make up your minds very quickly. My time is up on the 24th.'

'We could make up our minds in half an hour, if Clement would consent,' answered Mrs. Dulcimer, 'It would be such a delightful change for Beatrix. Mr. Namby has been recommending her a change of air and scene for ever so long; and it is much too cold for the sea-side. A week in Hampshire would do her a world of good.'

'Pray do not think of me,' said Beatrix, 'I had rather go home while you are away.'

'I thought this was your home now, Beatrix,' remonstrated the Vicar.

'It is the only house that has ever seemed like home,' the heiress answered, sadly.

'Of course you will go with us, if we go,' exclaimed Mrs. Dulcimer. 'You are our adopted daughter, and we expect you to go everywhere with us. We don't even consult you. It is quite a matter of course. I have set my heart on seeing Culverhouse Castle, and the visit will be the very thing to do you good. I am sure Mr. Namby would say so if I asked him about it. So, Clement dear, if you would let Mr. Rodger do duty for just one Sunday, we might spend ten days at Culverhouse very easily.'

Mr. Rodger was the new curate, a painstaking youth, with sandy hair and a large round face like the setting sun.

Mr. Dulcimer was at first disinclined to listen to his wife's suggestions. The journey was long and expensive, and there seemed to be no justifiable reason for undertaking it; but the Vicar was an indulgent husband, and he was very fond of salmon fishing, so the discussion ended by his giving his consent, and it was arranged that he, and the two ladies should join Sir Kenrick at the castle two days after the young man's arrival there.

Beatrix consented to go to Culverhouse, just as she would have consented to go to Buxton, Harrogate, or Scarborough, if Mrs. Dulcimer had wished her to go there. That disgust of life which had taken possession of her, since the overthrow of her faith in Cyril, left her indifferent to all things. She let her maid pack a portmanteau, and get all things ready for the journey. The girl, Mary, who had waited upon her at the Water House, had accompanied her to the Vicarage. She was not an accomplished attendant, but she was faithful, and Beatrix liked her.

Culverhouse Castle was six miles from a railway station; one of its chief merits, as Kenrick asserted proudly. He was standing on the platform when the train arrived, and received his guests with as much enthusiasm as if he had not seen them for a year or so. He had a carriage ready to drive them across to Culverhouse.

It was a lovely drive in the spring evening, the sun setting behind the wooded hills, and all the

soft rustic scene steeped in warm yellow light.
Culverhouse was on the edge of the New Forest,
and the road from the station to the castle went
through a region of alternate pasture and woodland.
Meadows and banks were yellow with primroses;
the earliest ferns were showing their tender green;
the dog-violets shone like jewels amongst the grass;
and the woods were full of white wind-flowers that
shivered at every whisper of the April breeze.
To Beatrix it all seemed very lovely. She breathed
more freely in this unknown world, where nobody
had ever spoken evil of her. There was an infinite
relief in having left Little Yafford.

When Culverhouse Castle rose before them on
the other side of the river, Beatrix thought it the
loveliest place she had ever seen. The Avon
widened to a smooth lake, and beyond it rose
the grave old Gothic towers, like a castle in a fairy
tale. Beatrix turned to Kenrick, with the kindest
smile she had ever bestowed upon him.

'It is a delicious old place,' she exclaimed. 'I
cannot wonder that you are proud of it.'

Kenrick was delighted. His face glowed with

pride of race and love for the house of his birth. They were driving through the little village street, all the old men and women, young men and maidens, doing them obeisance as they passed. Then they crossed the bridge and drove under the gateway, which was a couple of centuries older than the castle itself, and a minute later Kenrick passed into the banquet-hall of his ancestors, with Beatrix on his arm. He had offered his arm to Mrs. Dulcimer, but that match-making matron had bidden him take care of Miss Harefield, so he had the happiness of leading Beatrix across the threshold. 'Jest as if they'd been married and he'd been a-bringin' she home,' old Betsy Mopson said afterwards to her husband, gardener and man-of-all-work. 'Her be a rare beauty, her be.'

Kenrick had done wonders in his two days of preparation. He had got in a brace of apple-faced young women, from the village, one a housemaid out of place, the other her younger sister, still on her promotion, but ready to do anything she was bidden. The old rooms had been furbished up. Traces of decay were still visible in every part

of the house, but dust and cobwebs had been
swept away, and a general air of freshness and
purity pervaded the good old rooms.

Beatrix was enraptured with everything. She
seemed to forget her sorrows amidst these new
surroundings. Her life had been spent in a prison-
house, and this first taste of liberty was sweet.
After all, perhaps, even for her, deserted and cast
off by the one man she had ever loved, life held
something worth having.

Kenrick led his young guest all round the
ruins next morning, before breakfast. They were
both early risers, and had found each other in
the garden before Mr. and Mrs. Dulcimer had
left their rooms. They went into the cloistered
quadrangle, where the roses flourished in summer-
time, and where now the wallflowers flashed
golden and ruby upon the old gray stones, with
colours as vivid as the stained glass that had
once filled the place with rainbow light. Kenrick
showed Beatrix the plan of the vanished abbey—
the nave here, the transept there, the chancel and
apse beyond. Everything was indicated by stones

embedded at intervals in the close-cropped turf, where the sheep browsed happily, unconscious of the sanctified splendour that had preceded them, the white-robed choir, and swinging censers, the banners and jewelled crosiers that had passed beneath the Gothic arches which had once spanned that fair pasture. Kenrick seemed as sorry for the evanishment of the abbey as if he had been a papist of the deepest dye.

'It is dreadful to think that a great part of the house is built out of the abbey stones,' he said. 'I sometimes wonder it doesn't tumble on our heads. But tradition says the monks of Culverhouse were lazy and ignorant, and that there was only one book, an ancient treatise upon Hunting and Fishing, found in this abode of monastic learning, when its treasures were confiscated.'

Beatrix had explored every inch of the grounds before the long-disused gong, which in days past had called poor lonely Lady Culverhouse to her anchorite repasts, sounded hoarsely from the hall. Mr. and Mrs. Dulcimer were standing in the porch, scenting the morning air, when Kenrick and his companion went in.

'How well the dear girl looks!' said the Vicar's wife; 'the change has done her good already. You are enjoying Culverhouse, are you not, Beatrix?'

'I am very glad to be away from Little Yafford,' Beatrix answered, frankly.

'In that case you ought never to go back,' said Kenrick.

'What a selfish remark!' exclaimed Mrs. Dulcimer, hypocritically. 'How do you suppose I am to exist without Beatrix, after having had her as my adopted daughter for the last three months?'

'What do you think of the weather for salmon-fishing?' asked the Vicar, contemplating the bright blue sky with a discontented look that was hardly becoming in a Christian. 'We could do with a little more cloud, couldn't we, Ken? But, as time is short, we must make the best of things. I shall expect you to set off with me directly after breakfast.'

'I shall be delighted,' answered Kenrick; but he did not mean to give up his day to salmon-fishing.

He contrived to set the Vicar going, in a spot where there was every chance of good sport, and then, under the pretence of having orders to give about the dinner, ran home across the low-lying water meadows like a boy let loose from school. He found Mrs. Dulcimer expounding the chief features of the mansion—which she had never seen before—to Beatrix, while Betty Mopson stood by in attendance upon them, and made a running commentary, in a Hampshire dialect, which was like a foreign language to the strangers from the north.

'Hah! Lady Culverhouse wur a good 'ooman,' said Mrs. Mopson. 'Thur bean't many like she. This be the room where hur died. Her wur a rale lady. And Sir Kenrick, him takes after she.'

Kenrick came in time to hear his praises. He sent Betty back to her kitchen.

'We shall not get a decent luncheon if you waste all your morning chattering here, Betty,' he said, and Betty departed, grinning and ducking, and with a fixed idea that the young lady with the dark 'haiyur,' was to be the next Lady Culverhouse.

Kenrick spent a happy day in attendance upon the two ladies. He forgot everything, in the intoxicating delight of the present, forgot that this holiday in life was to be of the briefest, and that a fortnight hence he was to be tossing off Gibraltar in a Peninsular and Oriental steamer. Beatrix seemed happy also, or, at least, she appeared to be in a condition of placid contentment which was not unpromising.

The Vicar was successful with his rod, and came home radiant. Betty Mopson had surpassed herself in the preparation of a substantial English dinner. Everything went smoothly and well with Sir Kenrick.

Next day he carried off his guests to see some of the lions of the neighbourhood—a fine old abbey church sorely neglected—a castle where luckless King Charles had spent a night in safe keeping. Beatrix, who felt the unreasoning pity which all young and generous minds feel for that weak-minded and ill-used Stuart, contemplated the gloomy stone walls as if they had witnessed the heroic doom of an early Christian martyr. Then came the long drive home, through the spring twilight, across woods which were like glimpses of Paradise.

So the week wore on, in simple pleasures which might have seemed tame and dull to those world-weary spirits of the Sir Charles Coldstream calibre, who have done everything, and found emptiness everywhere, but which were sweet and new to Beatrix Harefield. A faint bloom began to warm her clear olive cheek, the dark depths of her Italian eyes shone with a new light. Yet she had not forgotten Cyril Culverhouse, nor one drop in the bitter cup she had drained since her father's death.

One evening after dinner, while the golden glow was still warm in the west, Beatrix and her host found themselves alone together in the cloistered garden. Until this moment Kenrick had not said one word about his disappointed hopes. His conduct had been perfect. He had been full of flattering attentions for his young guest; he had anticipated her every wish, devoted every free moment of his day to paying her homage; but he had never put on the air of a lover, nor insinuated a hope that could alarm her with the idea that Culverhouse Castle was a trap in which she was to be caught unawares.

He had his views and his hopes all the same, in spite of her unqualified rejection a few weeks ago. And now 'she had been a guest in his house nearly a fortnight, and she seemed happier and brighter than he had ever known her. His brief span of delight was nearly at an end. In a few days his guests would depart, the steamer would sail, and he must go back to the weary drudgery yonder under the dense blue of a Bengal sky—the early drill—the monotonous days—the narrow society—the blank sense of exile from all that is best and brightest in life. If the game were to be won ever, it must be won quickly.

It may have been some soft influence in sky or earth, the magic of the hour, that moved him to take the awful plunge this evening. His chances

of being quite alone with Beatrix were few, and
this opportunity, which came by accident, might
be the last. However it was, he resolved to cast
the die.

This time he told no long story about his love.
He had said his say that March afternoon in the
Vicarage library. He only took Beatrix by the
hand as they stood idly side by side, looking
down at the wallflowers and polyanthuses growing
among the old gray stones—the capitals and bases
of columns that had fallen long ago, and said
earnestly,—

'Beatrix, I want you to be mistress of this
place. I will not say another word about my
love for you. I will not ask for your love. That,
I hope and believe, would come to me in good
time if you were my wife; for it would be the
business of my life to win it. I want you to
come and reign at Culverhouse. Let me be your
steward—your servant.'

'You place yourself too low and me too high,'
answered Beatrix, sadly. She had not withdrawn
her hand, and Kenrick's heart thrilled with a

new-born hope. 'You forget my tainted name.
Kind as the people here are to me, I dare say
there is not one among them who does not know
that I have been suspected of poisoning my
father.'

The pained look in her face told Kenrick how
bitter this thought was, and how ever present
in her mind.

'They know nothing except that you are the
loveliest and noblest of women,' said Kenrick.
'My love, my love, do not reject me. You can
give me fortune to restore the glory of a good
old name—to bring back to this place the pride
and hospitality and usefulness of days gone by—
and I can give you nothing in exchange, save love
and reverence. It is hardly a fair bargain, perhaps; yet I am bold enough to press my suit,
for I believe that you and I could be happy
together.'

After a pause of a few minutes, and a long-
drawn sigh, Beatrix answered him with a sweet
seriousness that to him seemed simply adorable.

'I had my dream of a very different life,'

she said, 'but that dream was rudely broken. I
like you, Sir Kenrick, because you have trusted
me ; I am grateful to you because you have never
let the evil thoughts of others influence your
mind against me. If you can be content with
liking and gratitude, I am content to be your
wife.'

There was a tone of resignation rather than
happiness in this acceptance, but it lifted Kenrick
into the seventh heaven of delight.

' Dearest, you have made me almost mad with
joy,' he cried. ' You shall never regret—no, love,
God helping me, you shall never regret your sweet
consent of this blissful evening.'

He drew her to his heart, and kissed the
tremulous lips, which shrank from him with an
involuntary recoil. How cold those lips were ! If
he had kissed her in her coffin that kiss could
hardly have been colder.

CHAPTER XIV.

'OH, BREAK, MY HEART!—POOR BANKRUPT, BREAK
AT ONCE.'

CYRIL CULVERHOUSE had entered upon a career of
unceasing toil. He had given himself scanty rest
or respite at Little Yafford, though it was a place
where most curates would have taken life easily;
but at Bridford he learned, for the first time, what
work means in an overcrowded, sorely neglected
manufacturing town. The ignorances and abuses
which he found rampant in those noisome back
slums and overcrowded alleys, lying hidden behind
the outward respectability of the high street, aroused
his indignation against a system that allowed such
things to be. He was no democrat; he had no
sympathy with would-be levellers; but it seemed
to him that there must be something out of joint
in the time, when such depths of social degradation
were left to their native gloom, while the gaslit

thoroughfare and the shriek of the railway engine testified to the march of improvement.

Soon after the arrival of Cyril Culverhouse at Bridford, the respectable inhabitants were startled by a series of letters in their leading newspaper, letters characterized by that noble eloquence which comes straight from a heart moved to indignation by the wrongs and sufferings of others. No man could feel his own griefs so keenly as this anonymous writer felt the miseries of his fellow-townsmen. With an unflinching hand he tore aside the curtain from those dens of infamy and ignorance which the citizens of Bridford were willing to ignore, or to speak of with a deprecating shrug, and an admission that Bridford was a very bad place. It had never occurred to anybody that it was his business to make the place better. No modern Peter the Hermit had arisen to call for a crusade against ignorance and vice. The Bridfordians were too hotly bent upon money-making to have time to spare for crusades of any kind. Those letters in the *Bridford Journal* did some good, and roused some citizens who had been as deeply slumberous as to the condition of their fellow-men as if they had been the pampered lackeys of the Sleeping Beauty, wasting a century in one after-dinner snooze, with a vaguely pleasant sense of repletion, afternoon sun, the lullaby of summer woods, and the drowsy hum of insects.

But it was not with his pen alone that Cyril worked. Wherever the state of things was worst he was oftenest to be found. That tall erect figure of his grew to be as familiar in the alleys and back slums of Bridford as the hawker with his stale and damaged wares, or the drunken factory hand reeling home after dark. Wherever he went he did good. He, whose voice had been grave and gentle at Little Yafford, here spoke in tones of thunder. He was fearless in reprobation of brutish cruelty and besotted self-indulgence. He was tender and compassionate as a woman to the weak and oppressed, the women and children. First he made himself feared, and then he made himself loved. Even the men—the burly hardened sinners—to whom he spoke home-truths unflinchingly,—even these ended by liking him.

'I loike 'im 'cos he ain't afeared on us,' said one

of these strayed lambs ; 'he'll coom into my place
and call me, like a pickpocket, and yet he knaws for
half a farthin' I'd oop wi' one o' my clogs and brain
'im.   He ain't afeared, bless you.   He puts me in
moind o' th' lion tamer wot cum along o' th' show.'

The parish church at Bridford was only just big
enough for a highly respectable congregation, people
who had 'top hats' and best bonnets, and who came
to church regularly every Sunday because it was the
right thing to do, and dissected their neighbours'
characters afterwards on their way home.   Here
Cyril felt the rough denizens of the slums and alleys
were not wanted.   There was no room for them.
They would have been put to shame by the best
bonnets and the sleek broadcloth.   He did at first
try to get them to go to church on a Sunday evening.
He organized week-day evening services, and instruction classes.· But even from these the factory
people hung back.   The old parish church, with its
shining oaken pews and brass chandeliers, was too
grand for them.   Then Cyril took round the hat
among the wealthy manufacturing 'families, some of
whom had been roused by those stirring letters in

the newspapers, and collected funds for a mission chapel. He began in a very humble way, by fitting up a large room that had once been a coffee-house, but had languished for want of appreciation, the community leaning to stronger liquor than tea or coffee. Here he had services and instruction classes four times a week, thinly attended at first; but by-and-bye the room came to be filled to overflowing, and Cyril began to think of building a chapel.

He had got thus far, working night and day, shutting out of his mind as much as possible all thoughts of himself, and the hopes that he had cherished and renounced, when he received a letter from his cousin Kenrick, which gave him more pain than anything that had ever happened to him; except Christian Harefield's death, and the train of circumstances attending upon it.

'*Culverhouse Castle, April 30th.*

'DEAR CYRIL,—I should not like a stranger to tell you of the most important event in my life, before you had heard of it from me.

'I sail for India the day after to-morrow, but I

go only for a year. One little year hence I shall
sell out, and come back to England to settle down
in my old home. I renounce all hope of military
distinction. Whatever ambition I may have will
take a new line. I am going to be married,
Cyril. The woman, who is, to my mind, loveliest
and most perfect among women, has promised to
be my wife. A year hence, all going well, Beatrix
Harefield and I are to be married, and I shall
bring to the old house the fairest mistress that ever
reigned over it.

'Is this to make any breach between you and me,
Cyril ? God forbid. You have retired from the race.
You must not be angry with me for going in to win.
I write lightly enough, but I feel deeply. I would
not willingly have come between you and your
chosen love ; but when you fell out of the running,
of your own choice, and deliberately renounced your
chance, I held myself free to woo and win Miss
Harefield, if I could. She was not easily won, but
every day of our acquaintance made me more intensely in earnest, and I think a man could hardly
desire to win so strongly as I did, and not end by

winning. She is all goodness, sweetness, and nobility; and she loves this place already almost as dearly as I do. Indeed, sometimes I think it is Culverhouse that has won her, and not I. But I am content, deeply content.

'I am going away for a year. That is part of our compact. By that time her mourning will be over. She will throw off her black robes and shine out as a bride. All the people round about have made up their minds from the beginning that she is to be Lady Culverhouse. The village children, the toothless crones, bob to her with that intent.

'Am I not a man to be envied, Cyril? In our boyish days, when good Mrs. Dulcimer used to say to me, "Kenrick, you must marry an heiress," I always answered No; for in those days I thought that marrying an heiress must mean marrying for money; but now the money comes to me joined with love so deep and true that fortune is but a feather-weight in the scale. Were my sweet one penniless I would as gladly marry her, and let Culverhouse Castle go to the dogs. This is no idle boast, Cyril. I mean it, and feel it at the bottom of my heart.

'And now, dear boy, be generous as you have ever been to a comrade who owns himself in all things your inferior. Write me one little line to tell me that this new happiness of mine shall make no barrier between you and me, that you are not angry with me for loving and winning the woman you might have won, but did not. Tell me this much, Cyril, and fill my cup of joy to overflowing, before I see the Wight fade into a blue speck upon the distant horizon.

'Your faithful friend and cousin,

'KENRICK CULVERHOUSE.'

Cyril sat for an hour with this letter crushed in his hand, motionless as if he had been turned into stone. She was lost to him for **ever**. Of his own deliberate act he had renounced her and let her go,— but the fact that he had lost her utterly had never come home to him till now. And innocent or guilty he must love her to the last beat of his heart. He was very sure of that now.

CHAPTER XV.

MR. and Mrs. Dulcimer and their ward went back to Little Yafford on the same day that saw Sir Kenrick's departure from Southampton in the Peninsular and Oriental steamer. The parting between the betrothed lovers was more serious than sentimental. Beatrix was touched by Kenrick's devotion, and grateful for his confidence, and there was a grave tenderness in her manner at parting which made him very happy, for it seemed to him the promise of a warmer feeling in the future.

'You will be thinking of me sometimes when I am away,' he said.

'Yes. You will be serving your country. I shall honour you for that.'

'If there is no war I shall sell out ten months hence, and be with you before the year is out. But if war should break out—and there is always some trouble cooking in the witches' caldron of Indian politics—it may be longer before we meet. You will not forget me, Beatrix. Your feelings will not change —if our separation should be longer than we anticipate.'

'I have given you my promise,' she said, with a noble simplicity that impressed him deeply. 'If you were to be away ten years instead of one year, there would be no difference. I should not break my word.'

'And you would remember—and love me ? ' he urged.

'I have not promised to love you,' she answered. 'I have only promised to be your wife.'

'Ah !' he sighed, 'that is different, is it not ? Well, dearest, the love must be won somehow. Perhaps if there is some hard fighting, and I come home with one arm the less, and a captaincy, you will think more of me. I shall think of you when I am storming a fort—if there should be any forts to storm.'

Then he took her in his arms, kissed the pale brow and tremulous lips, and gave her his farewell blessing, and so left her, full of hope. There never was man born who doubted his power to win a woman's love.

The Vicar and his wife were both anxious that Beatrix should remain at the Vicarage, but Beatrix had made up her mind that she ought to go back to the Water House. The old servants were all there; nothing had been altered since her father's death.

'I shall be tranquil and happy there,' she argued, when Mrs. Dulcimer tried to persuade her that she would be miserable. 'I shall have my books and piano, and shall work hard, and I shall be free to come and see you as often as you care to have me.'

'That would be always,' exclaimed Mrs. Dulcimer, who had been rapturously fond of Beatrix ever since the success of her matrimonial scheme. 'But, my love, you cannot possibly live alone. People would talk.'

Beatrix shuddered. Young as she was, she had had bitter experience of the power of evil tongues.

'I suppose I must have what Thackeray calls a sheep dog,' she said. 'As I have outgrown my governess I must have a companion. Would not Bella do?'

'No, dear, she is not old enough. It would be just the same as having no one. It will be only for a year, remember, Beatrix. A year hence you will be married, and your own mistress.'

'If there is no war, and if Kenrick comes home.'

'We will hope there will be no war. I shall be so proud and happy when I see you established at Culverhouse Castle. It was my idea, you know, long ago, before you or Kenrick dreamed of such a thing. Clement would never have thought of it ; but I saw from the very first that you and Kenrick were made for each other.'

Mrs. Dulcimer could not refrain from these little gushes of self-gratulation. This engagement of Sir Kenrick and the heiress was the first grand success that had come out of all her match-making. She had brought a good many couples together, occasionally for better, and often for worse ; but she had never before made such a match as this. She felt as if the whole thing were her sole doing. She felt herself the saviour of the Culverhouse family. When the mortgages came to be paid, it would be her work.

Beatrix answered not a word. She was always grave and silent when the absent Kenrick was talked about. Her heart could not respond to Mrs. Dulcimer's raptures. She liked Kenrick, and believed him noble and disinterested; but between such liking and glad unreasoning love there is a wide gulf.

'Yes, my dear,' pursued Mrs. Dulcimer, 'if you are obstinately bent on living at the Water House, you must have a person of middle age for your companion.'

'Then I should like a Frenchwoman who could not understand one word of English,' said Beatrix.

She had her reason for this strange desire. She remembered how Miss Scales's heart, or that piece of mechanism which does duty for a heart in the Scales tribe, had been set against her by the slanderous gossip of Little Yafford. Her new companion must be some one who could not talk or be talked to. The knowledge of foreign tongues at Little Yafford was happily at a minimum. Beatrix knew of no one except Bella Scratchell who could have spoken half a dozen sentences in decent French.

'You would like to improve yourself in the language,' said Mrs. Dulcimer. She always called French 'the language.' 'Well, dear, we must put an advertisement in the *Times*; but I'm afraid it will be difficult to get the superior kind of person to whom we could entrust you. Of course we must state that unexceptionable references will be required.'

The advertisement appeared, and brought a shower of letters upon Mrs. Dulcimer, giving occasion to much consultation between her and Beatrix, but among them all there was only one letter that gave Beatrix an agreeable idea of the writer. This came from a lady who had only just come to England, a childless widow, whose husband, a provincial journalist, had lately died, and left her in reduced circumstances, and who had come to London to try to make some use of her literary talents, only to find that literary talents were a drug in the market.

Beatrix liked the letter. The lady's references were satisfactory; so, after a little time lost in negotiation, Madame Leonard was engaged, and in due course appeared at the Water House.

Her appearance was not unpleasing to Beatrix.

She was a little woman, with light brown hair and dark brown eyes, small hands and feet. She was neatly dressed in black, and had the manners of a lady. Since society insisted upon her having a companion, Beatrix felt that she could get on as well with Madame Leonard as with anybody else; and Madame Leonard, who was evidently of a soft and affectionate nature, seemed delighted with Beatrix.

And now the Water House revived and brightened a little, and cast off the gloomy mantle that had hung over it through the last ten years of Christian Harefield's life. Mr. and Mrs. Dulcimer were often there. Bella Scratchell came and went as she pleased. Mr. and Mrs. Scratchell were invited to dinner occasionally, a condescension on Miss Harefield's part which almost overcame the hardworked lawyer's wife. It was a great privilege, no doubt, to visit at the Water House, but it involved fearful struggles beforehand in order to arrive at a toilette which should be worthy of the occasion. There was always something wanting, which it required all Bella's ingenuity to supply; and even when a happy result had been accomplished, poor

Mrs. Scratchell was not quite easy in her mind. She was so unaccustomed to dine out that she fancied some dreadful catastrophe must needs occur in her absence. The kitchen boiler might burst, or one of the smaller children might tumble into the fire, or scald himself with the kettle. That kettle was on Mrs. Scratchell's mind all the evening, even when she was smiling her company smile, and pretending to look at the engravings of Continental landscapes which Beatrix showed her after dinner. Even the Bay of Naples could not make her happy. Vesuvius reminded her too painfully of the kitchen boiler.

Beatrix found Madame Leonard a much more pleasant companion than Miss Scales. She was well read in her own language, and opened the wide world of classic and modern French literature to her pupil. They read together for hours, each taking her turn at reading aloud, and occupying herself in the interval with those delicate fancy works which women love.

Beatrix had let light and air into her mother's long unused rooms, and had taken possession of them for her own occupation. Nothing was disturbed. The daughter respected every detail of the rooms in which her mother had lived. It was her delight to keep all things exactly as Mrs. Harefield had left them.

So life went on, smoothly enough. Beatrix had no friends but the Dulcimers and the Scratchells. She carefully avoided all the 'best people' of Little Yafford, and received with a chilling reserve any advances that were made to her. To those whom she happened to meet at the Vicarage she was coldly civil, and that was all. If the Little Yaffordites were inclined to change their opinion about her, she gave no encouragement to any tardy gush of friendliness. She lived among them, but was not of them.

Miss Coyle retained her original views of Miss Harefield's character. Although strictly conservative by profession, as became a lady of ancient family, Miss Coyle had that kind of radicalism which consists in detesting every one better off than herself. She cherished a savage hatred of Beatrix, considering it an injustice in the distribution of wealth and power that a young woman of twenty should have ten thousand a year, and a fine old mansion at her sole disposal, while she, Dulcinea Coyle, should be cabined, cribbed, and confined in a cottage hardly big enough for a dovecote. True that the cottage was pretty, and that Miss Coyle was fond and proud of it ; but she would have been fonder and prouder of the Water House. Then Miss Coyle's income, being of that strictly limited order which renders the outlay of every sixpence a matter demanding foresight and careful calculation, naturally gave rise to comparisons with the revenue of Miss Harefield, which was large enough for the wildest extravagance.

This sense of a wrong adjustment of fortune, together with the fact of Mrs. Dulcimer's desertion, rankled in Miss Coyle's breast, and whereas other people in Little Yafford had left off talking or thinking about Christian Harefield's daughter, Miss Coyle continued to think about her, and took every convenient occasion of talking.

She was not even inclined to let Miss Harefield's companion go free. She happened to meet Madame Leonard one afternoon at the house of

Mrs. Scratchell, whom it was her custom to honour once or twice a year with a patronizing call. This was too good an opportunity to be lost. Miss Coyle rather prided herself on her acquaintance with the French language, in which she had been thoroughly 'grounded' five-and-forty years ago at an expensive boarding school. A good deal of the ground had given way during those forty-five years, but Miss Coyle did not know that. She was not at all afraid of addressing Madame Leonard, who had been carrying on a friendly conversation with Mrs. Scratchell, with the aid of a little interpretation by Bella.

Miss Coyle contrived to leave the Scratchell domicile in company with Madame Leonard.

'Je marcherai avec vous si vous n'avez pas d'objection,' began Miss Coyle, politely.

Madame Leonard declared that she would be charmed, ravished. Her manner implied that Miss Coyle's society was the one delight that she had longed for ever since her arrival in Little Yafford.

'Comment est Mademoiselle Harefield?' asked Miss Coyle.

Madame Leonard looked mystified. A stupid person evidently, Miss Coyle thought.

'Vous es la nouveau gouvernesse de Mademoiselle, n'est ce pas ?'

'Mais, oui, Madame, je suis heureuse de me nommer sa dame de compagnie.'

'Comment est elle ? Est elle plus facile dans son esprit ?'

Madame Leonard looked at a loss to comprehend this question.

'The woman doesn't understand her own language,' thought Miss Coyle. 'One of those Swiss-French-women one hears about, I dare say, who come from the top of Mont Blanc, and call themselves natives of Paris.'

And then she proceeded to explain herself at more length.

'Mademoiselle Harefield a été terriblement choquée par le mort de sa père. Il mourissait sous des circonstances peniblement suspicieux. Les gens de cette village ont dit des penible choses sur son mort. Je toujours desire à penser le mieux touchant mes voisinś, mais je confesse

que le mort de Monsieur Harefield était très suspicieux.　Mademoiselle Harefield est très riche.
Je ne souhaite pas de mal à elle, mais elle est une
jeune personne que je ne pouvais pas me justifier en
recevant dans mon maison.　Mon maison est très
petit, mais mes principes sont fortement fixés.'

This French _à la_ Stratford-atte-Bowe was
quite incomprehensible to Madame Leonard, but
she perceived dimly that Miss Coyle was not
friendly to Beatrix.　She bristled with indignation,
and replied in a torrent of rapid words which
might have been Chaldee for any comprehension
Miss Coyle had of their meaning, but the little
woman's gestures told that worthy lady how
much she had offended.

'Ah! vous es une temps-serveur comme vos
meilleurs,' she exclaimed, when the Frenchwoman
paused for breath.　'Mademoselle Harefield a
beaucoup de monnaie.　C'est assez pour vous.
Mais quand vous laissez elle je vous promis que
ce sera difficile pour vous à trouver un autre
situation.'

And with this assertion that Madame Leonard

was a time-server like her betters, and that she
would find it difficult to get another situation
when she left Miss Harefield, Miss Coyle put up
a brown holland parasol, which seemed made
expressly for virtuous poverty, and vanished in
a cloud of dust, like an angry goddess.

'But this woman is mad! I comprehend not
one word that she says,' exclaimed Madame Leonard
inwardly. 'Who can have anything to say against
that dear angel? She is an envious, a malignant.'

The warm-hearted little Frenchwoman had
too much delicacy to speak of Miss Coyle's out-
burst of spite to Beatrix. She was puzzled by it,
but in no wise influenced against her pupil, whom
she had taken to her heart.

CHAPTER XVI

I ONLY LEARNED TO DOUBT AT LAST.

THE summer came in all its glory, a splendid
summer for the wide airy corn-fields, where the
lark sang high in a heaven of cloudless blue, above
the broad ripples of tawny gold—a splendid summer
for Hyde Park and the green valley through which
Father Thames winds his silvern ribbon,—a delicious
summer for the rich and prosperous in the land, for
whom sunshine means pleasure; but a terrible
summer for the overcrowded manufacturing town of
Bridford, where a hot season meant fever and disease
in its most malignant form. In the seething boiling-
pot of those Bridford alleys the fair July weather
brought endless sorrow and trouble; and wherever
the trouble was worst and the sorrow heaviest Cyril
Culverhouse was to be found. Night after night he
was to be seen moving, quietly as a shadow, from
house to house, to sit for an hour reading the gospel

to some fever-parched sufferer whose dull eyes might
never see another sunset.   The days were not long
enough for his work at this woeful time.   He was
obliged to give at least half his nights, and very often
the whole of them, to his sad duties.

'If you don't take care, my dear fellow, you'll
knock yourself up,' remonstrated the port-winey
Vicar, shocked at his curate's hollow eyes and pale
cheeks.   'It's no use sacrificing yourself in this way.
We've the same thing every summer.   The ther-
mometer and the death-rate go up together.   Sanitary reform is what we want, Culverhouse.   We
Churchmen can do very little good.'

'We can only do our duty,' answered Cyril.   'I
am not afraid of fever.'

'Well, as a single man you can face it with less
scruple.   I should go a great deal more among these
poor creatures, but Mrs. Rollings is dreadfully nervous.   She is so frightened about infection.   With
our large family we are bound to be careful.   Even
the funerals make her anxious.   She won't let me
go near the children after I've buried a fever case.
It's a deplorable state of things.'

Cyril faced these deplorable things without fear or wavering. What had he to fear? It was such work as his soul loved. To be where he was most wanted, where the sky was darkest and his little lamp could be of most avail, that was his idea of a parish priest's mission.

No heathens worshipping their wooden fetish in flowery islands of the fair South Seas could be further away from the light than these lost sheep of Israel; and it was to such as these he felt himself especially sent.

And then for his life. Like Hamlet, he valued that at 'a pin's fee.' He would have asked no better gift from the gods than to die doing his duty—a soldier of the Church militant, struck down in hand-to-hand combat with the enemy. All things which make an earthly lot sweet and valuable to man were lost to this man. He loved, and had renounced the woman he loved. He loved her still, more dearly than ever in separation; and he knew that she was to be the wife of another. Of fortune or advancement in life he had no hope. The Church is a profession few men would choose, de-

siring either fortune or advancement.   He had
nothing to live for but his duty, and it would be
sweeter to him to die for that than to go on living
for it.

Every thought of Beatrix Harefield was pain ;
most painful of all was the thought that she would
think him mean and cowardly for his defection.   If
she was innocent she must scorn him for his doubt
of her.   If she was guilty she must deem him a
coward for refusing her remorse the shelter of his
love.   He remembered those lines of Moore's,—

'Come rest in this bosom, my own stricken deer,
Though the herd have fled from thee, thy home is still here.'

He had been like the herd, and had fled from
his beloved in the day of her shadowed fame.   He
thought of his defection with deepest regret ; yet it
seemed to him that to have done otherwise would
have been to palter with the truth.

This burden of sad thought made him more de-
sirous than another man would have been to lose his
sense of individual pain in the sorrows of others.
Parish priests had gone among the poor of Bridford

before Cyril's time, but none with such a ready ear for their complaints.

There was a small household which had a peculiar interest for Cyril. A widow and her son occupied a wretched back room in one of the wretched houses in a blind alley, a festering lane shut from the air and light by the overshadowing bulk of a huge factory, whereof the chimney, although under legal covenant to consume its own smoke, rained showers of blacks upon the surrounding neighbourhood, like the spray from a perennial soot fountain.

Nothing could be more squalid than the house in which Mrs. Joyce and Emmanuel Joyce, her son, lived. Their neighbours were no cleaner or tidier than the rest of the community. There was the usual all-pervading odour of fried herrings, and decaying cabbage-leaves. The back yard, nine feet by six, was a horror to stop the nose at. The eye was offended by hideous sights, the ear was outraged by foulest language, and yet in this leper-house there was one spot which the infected air of the place had not tainted.

Mrs. Joyce and her son had contrived to impart neatness and order, and even a certain respectability to the one small back room on the ground-floor, which constituted their house and home. Very small were the means by which they had achieved this result, but the result was palpable to every eye.

'It's well to be them,' said the mother of many children, peering with longing eyes into the neatly kept parlour. 'If I had no childer I might make my place tidy; but where there's childer there's muck.'

Emmanuel Joyce was a cobbler by trade. Now of all trades perhaps cobbling is about one of the most unpleasant with which to be brought into immediate contact, but Emmanuel, who paid his weekly rent punctually, and was in that respect a striking exception, had obtained leave to erect a small shed in the angle of the yard next his window. This shed was looked at with envious eyes by some of his fellow-lodgers, and talked of invidiously as an encroachment; but here Emmanuel squatted at his work in all weathers, and here he kept his tools, and those crippled boots and shoes upon which he exercised his healing art.

In the parlour he had contrived to build a couple of enclosed beds on the Scotch principle, which, though wanting in airiness, were tidy and decent. At night a curtain divided the one small room into two, and by day this curtain drawn back and neatly looped up, made one of the decorations of the neat parlour. A tall stand of flower-pots, Emmanuel's dearest care, screened the loathesomeness of the yard, and made the one window a bank of foliage and gay colour. The shabby odds and ends of furniture shone with the beeswax and labour which Mrs. Joyce bestowed upon them in the intervals of her plain sewing. There were cheap prints on the wall above the mantelpiece, and on each side of the fireplace there were three deal shelves, containing Emmanuel's much-prized collection of books, all picked up at odd times from the rubbish-box of a second-hand bookseller, and rebound and furbished by Emmanuel's own dexterous hands.

'My son is a great reader,' Mrs. Joyce said proudly, during Cyril's first visit. 'He keeps the money other young men spend on beer to buy books with.'

Cyril went over to the shelves and looked at the books. Their character told him more about Emmanuel Joyce's way of thinking than the mother would have cared to tell. There was an odd volume of Shelley, another of Keats, a Milton, and a Shakespeare. So much for the poets. Then came Rousseau's 'Confessions,' in English, Tom Payne's 'Age of Reason,' and a dozen other books all more or less infidel in their tendency.

'Your son goes to church, I hope?' said Cyril, after he had examined the books.

The widow hung her head, and began to fidget with the corner of her print apron.

'I'm sorry to say he's no church-goer, sir. It's his only fault. He was brought up very strict, a little too strict, perhaps. We were chapel people in my husband's lifetime, and I think he was a bit too hard on the boy. It turned Emmanuel's stomach against religion. And now he's got hold of all sorts of queer ideas, and he puts 'em into poetry. It's beautiful poetry to listen to, full of book learning. My son reads it to me of an evening; but it soars too high for me sometimes, I can't quite follow the ideas.'

' I should like to have a little talk with your son,' said Cyril.

'Ah, sir, if you could but bring him to think better of his Maker, and his Maker's way of managing this world, it would be a blessed thing,' exclaimed the widow. ' That's all my son needs to make him as perfect as any human creature ever was upon this earth. He's the best of sons, he's the honestest, soberest, industriousest of young men. But it makes me shudder sometimes to hear him talk; that bold, as if he'd been up among the stars, and knew the way they're worked. I believe it all comes of too much learning.'

' Or too little,' suggested Cyril.

' Oh, sir, you wouldn't say that if you was to see the books he devours. He belongs to the Mechanics' Institute, and there isn't a learned book they've got that he hasn't gone right through. He don't care for stories and such like. He calls them fiddle-faddle. But he'll sit up half the night over a learned book, and then he puts his ideas into poetry.'

Cyril was warmly interested. To begin with, a cobbler who read Keats and Shelley stood out prominently from the ruck of cobblers. It has been said that cobblers, as men whose habits are sedentary and meditative, have a natural leaning to infidel opinions; but Cyril did not believe this. He did not believe that meditation must needs engender doubt. He who wrote the divinest work ever penned by an uninspired writer, 'The Imitation of Christ,' must have been of all men the most meditative. And did not Bunyan's twelve years of imprisonment in Bedford gaol bear fruit in 'The Pilgrim's Progress?' a book that has done more to popularize Christianity than all the writings of all the bishops who ever wore lawn. Cyril could not see any reason why cobbling and Christian belief should be incompatible.

'I will call and see your son,' he said, Emmanuel happening to be out of the way on his first visit.

He called the following evening, a dismal rainy evening, when he thought the cobbler, as a man not given to spend his time in tap-rooms, likely to be at home. Nor was he disappointed. Emmanuel Joyce was sitting at a little table, drawn close to the bank of flowers in the window, poring over a page of Carlyle's 'Latter Day Pamphlets,' his elbow on the table, his thin hand entangled in his long hair, and with far from a comfortable expression of countenance.

That Thomas Carlyle is a grand and noble writer, no one who has ever read his 'French Revolution,' his 'Life of John Sterling,' and his 'Hero Worship,' could have the insolence to deny; but he is a writer demanding a considerable expenditure of brain power on the part of his readers; and for a worker who has been sitting in a cramped position all day mending shoes, to find himself lost among the Immensities, or vainly endeavouring to grapple with Phantasmal Captains, Ineptitudes, and other strange creatures, is hardly the most refreshing form of mental solace after physical labour.

Mrs. Joyce was sewing on the other side of the little table, wasting her eyesight in order to economize her candle. Mother and son rose at Cyril's entrance, and the widow brought forward the best chair, a battered old easy chair, which her son had neatly covered with bright-looking chintz, for the visitor.

Emmanuel was tall, thin, and pale, with hollow cheeks and a projecting forehead, under which shone darkly bright eyes, large and bulbous. His lips were thin, his chin indicated a firmness of character verging upon obstinacy. It was an interesting face, but not altogether a pleasant one, save when the young man spoke to his mother, and then his countenance was lighted by a smile which made it beautiful.

'Mother told me you'd been to see her, sir,' he said. 'She took it very kindly that you should spare time to sit down and chat a bit with her, especially as you didn't leave a tract behind you.'

'You don't like tracts,' said Cyril, smiling at

the energy with which the last sentence was spoken.

'I detest them.'

'Yet I think the book you are reading is something in the form of a tract,' speculated Cyril, whose quick eye had caught the title of Carlyle's book.

'It is not a religious tract, sir. It appeals to man's highest faculties—it kindles all that is best and greatest in his soul—but it does not pelt him with Scripture texts, or tell him that he is by nature a reprobate and castaway, judged and doomed before he was born.'

'Do you think the Bible tells a man that?'

'Yes, sir, it does. The Bible texts that were flung at my head in my childhood and boyhood were all to one purpose. They told me that I was a vessel of wrath, and that I was doomed to the burning. When I was eighteen years of age I began to think for myself.'

'You began to work out your own salvation with fear and trembling.'

'No, sir. I had read Shelley's "Queen Mab," by that time, and I had my own ideas of the justice of

my Creator. If He were just He would not create
me for misery either here or hereafter. And then I
looked round me and saw a world that reeked with
human misery and divine injustice.'

'Stop!' cried Cyril. 'Were this world the end of
our life the differences in the fortunes of mankind
might imply injustice in the Ruler of this world;
but the balance is to be struck elsewhere—the day of
reckoning is to come, when each man shall reap the
reward of his works, whether they be good or evil.'

'Am I to take your word for all that?' asked
Emmanuel, his projecting eyes shining with a fierce
light. 'You are like the rest of them. One after
another they have come to me—Church of England,
Wesleyans, Baptists, Ranters — all with the same
dogmatic assertions. My own senses tell me that
this world teems with suffering and wrong. Am I
to take the other story on hearsay?'

'Have you not seen something more than suffering and wrong?' argued Cyril 'Have you not seen
that even in this brief mortal life—which true be-
lievers regard as but a troubled passage to eternal
peace—have you not seen that even here men reap

as they have sown ? To the sober man health and
tranquillity ; to the drunkard disease and early death.
To the honest man the world's respect ; to the reprobate the bitter cup of shame. This little room we
sit in bears the evidence of your sober, industrious
life. Where is the injustice here ? Now and then
we see a good man struggling with calamity—tried
as Job was tried—chastened as David was chastened
—but his struggles are an education for heaven ;
and could we but see rightly we might regard him as
a chosen servant of God.'

' And what of your hospitals for incurables, filled
with beings created only to suffer ? '

' You have never visited one of those hospitals,
or you would know that among those sufferers
there are many whom heaven has gifted with a
patience that makes life almost happy, and a faith
that fills even their hours of pain with hope.'

' Dreamers and enthusiasts all,' said Emmanuel.

' Amongst them are some who have talents that
make life interesting—or even genius that lifts them
up above the common earth and creates for them
a world of their own. We cannot measure our

fellow-men's misery or happiness, any more than
we can measure the goodness and justice of God.
Some of the most unhappy of men are those to
whom fortune has given all good things.'

'What do you deduce from this?'

'That if we could know the hearts and minds
of all men as God knows them we should not accuse
our Maker of injustice. He has given us the
highest of all gifts, understanding and free will.
It is for us to work out our redemption with these.'

'You believe in free will?' asked Emmanuel.

'As I believe in God's justice.'

'My father was a Calvinist. He believed himself one of the elect, and his fellow-men, mostly,
outside the pale.'

'You were brought up in that gloomy faith—
the faith of that hard good man who had love and
mercy neither for himself nor his fellow-men—
who put an honest woman in jail for dancing at
her kinsman's wedding—and condemned a brother
theologian to the stake for differing in opinion with
him. Well, I can hardly wonder that your mind
has taken a distorted view of Christianity, for

though a Calvinist may be a very good man, I doubt his being a pleasant man, or being able to make his faith sweet and pleasant to others. But if you will accept Christ's Christianity for your guide—if you will look to Christ's heaven as your goal—you will find no thorns in your path.'

And then, warming with his subject, Cyril spoke strongly and earnestly of gospel truth as he believed it—the unsophisticated teaching of Christ. Emmanuel Joyce listened, and liked to hear, but his opinions were not to be shaken in an evening. He had too long cherished and cosseted the demon of infidelity, to be able to thrust the foul fiend out of doors at a moment's warning.

'Come whenever you can spare an hour,' he said, when Cyril was going away. 'I like to hear you talk.'

'I will come as often as I can; but on one condition.'

'Name it.'

'That you come to church.'

'I'll come to hear you preach. I'm never above hearing a good preacher.'

'Come, that you may learn to pray,' answered Cyril. 'Life is a barren waste without that link between earth and heaven—the Jacob's ladder of prayer, upon which angels are continually ascending and descending.'

CHAPTER XVII.

THE ONLY SON OF HIS MOTHER.

AFTER that first interview Cyril saw Emmanuel Joyce often. His duty took him nearly every day to that fœtid alley where the cobbler contrived to grow his flowers, and to maintain a semblance of prettiness in his narrow dwelling. Whenever the curate had half an hour to spare in his daily round he spent it with Emmanuel, and their talk was generally of spiritual things; for, like most unbelievers, Joyce loved to discuss the religion he pretended to abjure.

One day when Emmanuel had quoted one of the most appalling passages in 'Queen Mab,' Cyril startled him by asking,—

'Do you know that Shelley was a lad of eighteen when he wrote those lines, and that the poem was published without his consent? You quote it to sustain your arguments with as much confidence as if it were the work of wisdom as mature as Bacon's or Pascal's.'

Emmanuel blushed.

'He was a boy in years, perhaps, but a man in genius,' he said.

'Granted. Shelley was a marvellous boy, with all Chatterton's precocity, and much more than Chatterton's spirituality. If the light of his genius led him astray, it was not the less light from heaven. I doubt not if Shelley had lived to be old he would have learned to believe in much that seemed foolishness to his young imagination. Do you ever read Tennyson?'

'Tennyson is too tame for me.'

'Take my advice and read him. He is not so great a poet as Shelley, but he is a greater teacher. He and Victor Hugo are the two great moralists of the age; and I would put Tennyson higher than Hugo, because his ethics are of a graver and calmer cast. I will bring you my Tennyson to-morrow.'

'You are too good,' said Emmanuel, touched by the curate's tone of equal friendship.

He went to hear Cyril preach, and listened with delight. He was willing to accept his new friend as a great moral teacher, but he was not willing to surrender his infidel opinions. He had hugged them too long. They were his hobby, as dear to him as a gallery of pictures to a wealthy connoisseur, or a cabinet of old china to a fine lady. But although the citadel had not yet yielded, its foundations were considerably weakened. After a fortnight's acquaintance with Cyril, the cobbler took his mother to church regularly every Sunday, much to the widow's delight. It was the only happiness that had been wanting in her simple laborious life, to go to church leaning on her son's arm.

So things went on till the middle of the summer. Emmanuel had left off reading infidel books, won altogether by the curate's sympathy. He stuck to his opinions, but he read the books Cyril chose for him, and enlarged the range of his ideas. Hitherto he had devoured books ravenously, but had not digested or absorbed their contents. Now he read in a methodic manner, and grouped his subjects, under Cyril's advice. He had supposed that all hard reading meant useful reading, but Cyril showed him that the best books were generally the easiest to read and remember.

One day when Emmanuel began a theological discussion the curate abruptly stopped him.

'I am not going to talk to you about religion any more,' he said.

'Why not?'

'Because it is useless and unprofitable, harmful even, for both of us. I have said all I have to say about sacred things, and I have failed to convince you. I will not talk of the gospel for the sake of argument, and with a man who has made up his mind to reject gospel truth. Let us talk of literature, politics, anything you like, except religion. I am warmly interested in the growth of your mind.'

'And you do not refuse to hold any communication with me because I am an infidel. You do not thrust me from you with loathing?'

'Assuredly not. I pity you too much.'

'You must be a man of very liberal opinions.'

'My Master was a Man of liberal opinions.'

'Yes, He sat at meat with publicans and sinners, the despised and the oppressed. He was the greatest, noblest, purest Man that ever lived, the wisest Teacher. If you claimed no more for Him than that——'

'We claim a great deal more than that; but I am not going to discuss these things. Tell me how you like Tennyson.'

'Better and better the more I read him.'

'Just so. I don't think anybody ever thoroughly likes Tennyson at the first reading.'

They went on to talk of the Laureate, and Cyril was surprised and pleased by the justice of the cobbler's criticism. Emmanuel was touched by the curate's forbearance. He expressed himself warmly when Cyril was taking leave of him.

'You are a man in a thousand,' he said. 'You are not liberal in words only, but in acts. One would suppose that in your eyes I should be an outcast—a Pariah—Anathema Maranatha.'

'You are a man,' answered Cyril, 'and your soul is precious in my esteem.'

Now came dark days for the pestiferous slums and putrescent lanes which surrounded and hemmed in the high street and market-place of Bridford, like a foul network of brick and mortar, shutting out the fresh sweet breezes that sweep over wood and pasture, moor and corn-field, and all the spicy summer odours of wild herbs and flowers. Mysteriously, scarce anyone knowing where the rumour first began, there arose the cry that cholera was in Bridford. People stood at the street corners, and on the doorsteps, telling one another of this fatal visitant, with awe-stricken faces and hushed voices. They were accustomed to small-pox, they were but too familiar with typhus and typhoid, which two fatal diseases the great Jenner was just then seeking to differentiate. But cholera was a foe that came but seldom, and when he came was scathing as that dark angel of the Lord before whose burning breath the host of Sennacherib melted like snow. They had had cholera in the fatal year of '32. It had revisited them in '47—and now, stricken with an awful dread, they clustered in little groups at the street corners, at the baker's, at the close little dingy shops that sold everything, and in which the atmosphere was pervaded with subtly blended odours of cheese, blacking, pickled onions, chicory, lucifer matches, candles, bacon, firewood, and red herrings. There was a general exodus of all the well-to-do people of Bridford. They packed their trunks in a feverish hurry, and carried their children off to the sea, whereby all the accessible watering-places were sorely overcrowded, and a fertile crop of typhus and scarlatina was grown in close lodgings and sewer-scented bedchambers; so much so that it was afterwards asserted that those who stayed at home, and faced the perils of cholera, and did a good deal to help their poorer neighbours, fared better than those more cautious spirits who fled before the face of the foe.

Cyril worked day and night. He had studied surgery in Paris in one of his long vacations, and had gone about among the London hospitals in order to be of use in cases of emergency. He was now a valuable aid to the overworked parish doctor and his pallid assistant. The disease had spread fast among the crowded tenements under the shadow of the great chemical factory. Those fumes of sulphur and oxalic acid which poisoned the air of heaven in this locality proved no antidote to the cholera poison· There had been a good many deaths already. Cyril hunted the parish officers to accomplish such sanitary improvements as might be effected on the spur of the moment; but the whole neighbourhood was a nest of rottenness. There was not a drain that did its duty, or a sewer that did not breathe forth pollution by day and night. The funeral bell sounded all day long, and the faces of the people were pale and worn with an ever-present fear.

Emmanuel Joyce went on with his daily work, and his nightly studies. He wrote dismal verses about the cholera fiend and his victims, and was more than ever inclined to question the justice and benevolence of his Creator.

'It isn't for myself I'm afraid,' he said to Cyril, who had scanty leisure now for literary discussions, but who looked in at Mrs. Joyce's parlour once a day for five minutes' friendly chat. 'A man can die but once. I'm no more afraid of sudden death than a soldier is when he stands in his place in the ranks and knows that the next shot may be for him. But I can't help feeling for the poor creatures round about — the mothers taken from their young children—the hard-working fathers carried off, and their little ones left to starve.'

'It is hard, I grant,' said Cyril. 'But there is some good in all evil things. This dreadful outbreak may arouse the corporation of Bridford from their wicked apathy. We shall have sanitary reform, perhaps, after this awful warning.'

'Ay, they'll shut the stable door when the steed's stolen,' retorted Emmanuel, bitterly.

A few days later a death occurred in the house in which the Joyces lived. Cyril found the widow sitting with her work in her lap—she whose needle was rarely idle—pale, and crying silently.

'Oh, sir,' she sighed, 'my poor Emmanuel, my blessed, well-beloved son!'

'Dear Mrs. Joyce, is anything amiss with him? Is he ill?' asked Cyril, alarmed.

'No, sir—not yet. But oh, I am full of fear! The poor woman on the third floor—the young mother with the two children—you know—you were

with her last night. She's gone, sir. Only taken
yesterday morning, and gone this afternoon. A clear
case of Asiatic cholera, the doctor says. Who can
tell if my boy may not be the next?'

'My good soul, you will be the next if you fret
and frighten yourself like this. Does not God take
care of us all? Those who are taken are in His
keeping as truly as those He leaves behind. In life
or death we are with Him. Why should Emmanuel
be the next? He is sober and cleanly. He is better
cared for in every way than his neighbours.'

'Oh, Mr. Culverhouse, I love him so, he is all
the world to me. I could not live without him. I
have watched him grow up, as a child watches the
one flower in his little garden. Every day and hour
of his life has been precious to me. My only grief
has been that he should set his face against the
Bible. And now perhaps God is angry with him—
God must be angry at unbelief—and will snatch him
away from me.'

'That would be to punish you. God is all just.
He will give your son time to grow wiser.'

'Oh, sir, it is not always so. 'The wicked man is

cut off in the day of his iniquity. My son has
denied God, and may be smitten in his pride. The
poor young mother taken away from her babies, one
that can only just crawl, and the other six weeks
old ! Why should Heaven pity me more than those
babies ? '

'Because the loss must be harder for you. Some
kind soul will care for the babies.'

'True, sir, one of them was laughing and crowing
an hour ago. They don't know what death means.
But Emmanuel is my all. At night when he lays
down his book and talks to me for a little bit, I sit
and drink in his words as if they were wine, warming
and strengthening me. His poetry seems grander
to me than any other poet's. Yes, grander than
Milton or Shakespeare. I think God meant him
to be great.'

'I believe God meant him to be good.'

'Oh, Mr. Culverhouse, my mind is full of care
when I think of him. My husband believed that
some were chosen vessels of wrath. I have sometimes fancied that Emmanuel must be such a one.
To be so gifted, and yet to deny God ! To be so

good to me—the best and kindest of sons—and yet
to be stubborn against his God. I cannot understand it.'

'Can you not understand the case of a man to
whom Heaven has given a searching and inquiring
spirit—a mind not satisfied to be taught by others—
wanting to find out everything for itself? Such a
man, not having searched deep enough, may be still
in the dark ; but when he has lived longer, and
thought more, the light will come. Be sure of
that.'

'Do you believe that, Mr. Culverhouse ?'

'Honestly. I give Emmanuel another year for
his infidel opinions, and at the end of that time
I expect to see him testifying to his belief in
Christianity, like the apostle Paul, as ardent in
faith as he has been ardent in disbelief.'

'What comfort you have given me !' sighed the
widow.

Cyril went away touched by the mother's intense
love, deeply anxious for the safety of both mother
and son in that infected house. If he had been rich
enough he would have sent both off to some inland

village, far from the smoke of cities and the fumes of
factory chimneys. But he had drained his purse in
giving a little help in cases where help was most
bitterly needed. For one moment there flashed
across his mind the thought of what he might have
done to help these people, if Beatrix Harefield's fortune
had been his. What sunshine he could have carried
into dark places—what comfort, relief, ease of mind,
sanitary improvements—blessings of education and
moral enlightenment—better dwellings, hopefulness
everywhere. Money would have done all this, and
the woman he loved would have given him her
wealth freely for these things. And now the wealth
was useless and idle, and he and the woman he
loved were unlike unhappy. His purse was empty;
he could give Emmanuel and his mother nothing
but friendship and pity. He saw them every day,
though the continual calls upon his time made every
moment precious.

Unhappily Mrs. Joyce had not the firmness of
soul that can face a danger near at hand. She was
nervous and full of fear. She had all manner of
petty devices for keeping the enemy at bay. She,

who had never been given to gossip, now lingered at the chandler's shop, to talk to her neighbours, to hear the latest evil tidings, or to get the last specific which quackery had invented against the disease. Emmanuel's life was made a burden to him by his mother's care. She wanted him to take half a dozen different concoctions in a day. His affection yielded, while his common sense revolted.

'I haven't the least belief in these messes, but I'll take anything to oblige you, mother,' he said.

By and by the widow wondered to see her son's appetite begin to languish.

'I think those concoctions you give me are the cause of it,' he said, when his mother bewailed this alarming symptom. 'They sicken my stomach.'

'Oh, Emmanuel, everybody knows that sarsaparilla is strengthening, and ought to give you an appetite; and then there's the iron and the bark I got from the chemist's for you.'

'Yes, and the dandelion tea, and the ground-ivy.'

'That was to sweeten your blood, Emmanuel.'

'Mother, there was nothing the matter with me, and if you want me to take preventives against cholera, why can't you be contented with simple things? Mr. Culverhouse says that a tea-spoonful of common salt taken daily with one's food is the best preventive ever discovered, and that wouldn't make me turn against my dinner, as your ground-ivy and such like rubbish does.'

Hereupon the widow began to cry.

'I'm so anxious about you, Emmanuel,' she said.

'And so am I anxious about you, mother, but I don't worry you nor myself. What's the use? Here we are, rank and file, like soldiers, and the shells are exploding round us on every side. We may get hit, or we may not. There are survivors after all great battles. Think of those old fellows we have seen who were all through the Peninsular war. How many times must they and death have been within an inch of each other! We are no worse off than they were.'

The tolling of the funeral bell came like a full stop at the end of Emmanuel's speech.

One of Mrs. Joyce's ideas for the preservation

of her son's health—of herself she thought no more than if she had been invulnerable—was to get him as much as possible out of the tainted neighbourhood he lived in. She urged him to abandon his evening studies, and to take long walks into the country, she going with him. The young man humoured this fancy as he would have humoured any wish of his mother's, and the two used to set out after working hours on a rural tramp. The country, or anything pretty in the way of rustic scenery, was not easily reached from Bridford. Long dusty high roads, bounded by uninteresting fields of mangel, or turnips, had to be traversed before the weary pedestrian arrived at anything rural or refreshing to the senses. Emmanuel and his mother had both a keen love of the beautiful, and they overwalked themselves nightly in the endeavour to reach some green hill-side or wooded dell they knew of. The evenings were sultry and oppressive. More than once the wayfarers were caught in a thunder-shower, and went home wet to the skin. Altogether this precautionary measure of Mrs. Joyce's was about the worst thing she and her son could have done. The end was fatal. One night Emmanuel was seized with racking pain, and the usual symptoms of Asiatic cholera.

The parish doctor came early in the morning. Yes, there was no room for doubt, it was another case. The widow heard his opinion with a stony calmness. All her fussy anxiety seemed gone. Her pale set face betokened a despair too deep for words. She sat by her son's pillow. She wiped the drops of agony from his drawn face. She obeyed to the letter every direction the doctor had given her.

'How good you are!' she said once, when she had seen the struggle between fortitude and pain, 'how patient! Oh, my dear one, surely this is Christian patience. I know it. I feel it. At heart you are a Christian.'

'I have tried to live an honest life,' the sick man answered, feebly. 'I have tried to keep my name fair in the sight of men—and to do as much good as I was able to my neighbours.'

'That is Christianity, my dear. If you would but acknowledge——But no, I won't talk to you now. God will have mercy. He will spare you—for me—for me. And then your heart will be melted and you will turn to Him.'

' Mother, if I should be taken away,' Emmanuel said later, ' I know Mr. Culverhouse will be good to you. You will not be friendless.'

' Not friendless! I have no friend but you. The earth would be empty for me if you were gone. Oh, my boy, my boy, do you think that I could go on living without you ?'

Cyril overheard these two speeches. He had knocked gently, and, receiving no answer, had softly opened the door. The neighbours, a family of nine, in the front room, had told him of Emmanuel's state.

' Oh, sir,' cried the widow, turning to him with streaming eyes, ' it has come. You know how I dreaded it—how I have prayed against it. I thought God would have mercy, that the scourge would pass by this door, as the angel of death passed by the doors that were sprinkled with the blood of the Lamb. But He has been deaf to my prayers.'

' He is never deaf to prayer, though He may

not give us the answer we desire,' said Cyril, gently.
'Do not give way to despair. With God's grace
your son will recover, as so many have done.'

'But how many have died!' said the widow,
sadly, as she resumed her seat by her son's pillow.

Cyril stayed for more than an hour, comfort-
ing both the sick man and his mother by his presence. He said very little to Emmanuel, for the
sufferer was in no state to talk or to be talked to.
It was one of those cases in which a death-bed
repentance—a calm survey of past errors and sins—
a deliberate act of allegiance to God—was not to
be expected. The sinking soul might clutch at the
cross held aloft before those dim eyes, as a drowning man catches at the rope flung out to him at
his last extremity; but any act involving thought,
any calm reception of divine truth, was impossible.
To Cyril's eye the young man seemed already sinking. He opened his book by and by without a
word of preface, and read those chapters of St.
John's gospel which contain Christ's parting address
to His disciples—words whose pathetic minor seems
to breathe sad sweetness into dying ears. Emman-

uel's face brightened as he heard. He remembered
how he had loved those chapters long ago, when
he had read them at his mother's knee, before
his father's severity and the hard ascetic life had
made all religious reading hateful to him.

'Yes,' he murmured presently, in an interval of
pain. 'That is a lovely farewell. Those used to
be your favourite chapters, mother.'

'They are so still, dear. I have never tired of
them.'

Cyril left with a heavy heart, promising to call
in the evening, at the hour when he would be
likely to meet the doctor. That anguish-wrung
countenance of the widow's haunted him all day
long. In the places where he went there was little
else but sorrow, but there seemed to him to be no
burthen like unto this burthen of hers—a grief and
a desolation beyond speech.

'He was the only son of his mother, and she
was a widow.' Those words were continually in
his mind. For that one widow—blessed and chosen
above all other afflicted women—God upon earth
worked one of His greatest miracles. Thrice only

in His earthly pilgrimage did He exercise that ineffable power—and on this occasion it seemed
exercised on the impulse of the moment. God's
human heart had been touched by this entirely
human grief. He did not say to the widow—as
His servants now say—'Rejoice, for your son is in
heaven.' He gave her back her son upon earth.

Cyril was heavy at heart, for he had seen every
cause for fear in Emmanuel Joyce's condition.

'If it were my life, now, that was in jeopardy,
it would matter very little,' he said to himself.
'Who is there to be sorry for me? My cousin
Kenrick would be grieved, perhaps, in a mild degree, to hear of my death; but it would make very
little difference in his life. This poor woman's
existence will be desolate if she loses her son.
There will be nothing left her. Hard to break the
chain of love when poverty and loneliness have
made each link so strong.'

The twilight was closing in when Cyril went
back to the room where Emmanuel Joyce was
lying, in an agony that looked like the throes of
death. The widow's ashen face indicated a know-

ledge of her son's peril. She tried to speak,
but could not. She could only hold out her cold
tremulous hand to the human friend of whose pity
she felt assured, and look at him with wild despair-
ing eyes. He pressed her hand gently, and sat
down by the bedside to watch the struggle, while
he waited for the doctor's coming.

'You have done everything?' he inquired.
'Yes, I am sure of that.'

The room had a stifling odour of laudanum and
brandy. The sick man's pinched and livid face,
hollow sunken eye sand brow bedewed with death-
like dampness made Cyril apprehend the worst. The
hands grasping the coverlet were shrunken and
wrinkled, the skin shrivelled like a washerwoman's
after her day's labour. The oppressed respiration,
the cold breath which chilled the curate's cheek as he
bent over his dying friend, alike inspired fear. Yet
the brain remained unclouded all the while, and the
hollow voice hoarsely whispered grateful acknowledgment of Cyril's kindness. Never had Emmanuel
Joyce been calmer in mind than in this dark hour.
He waited with resignation for recovery or death.

It was more than an hour before the parish doctor appeared.

'There are so many cases,' he said, apologetically.

And then he looked at the patient with a calm business-like air that tortured the mother's heart. He felt the pulse, put his hard hand upon the clammy brow.

'He's very bad to-night.'

'Worse than he was this morning?' asked the widow, hoarsely.

'Ever so much worse.'

'And you said this morning that he was in danger.'

'My good woman, I'm very sorry for you,' said the doctor, shrugging his shoulders, 'but it's a very bad case. Frankly, it's hopeless. There's no use in deceiving you. The young man is dying.'

No cry of despair came from the mother's parched lips. She made no moan, but only crouched by her son's bed, clasping him in her arms, as if she would have held him back from death by the sheer force of maternal love. She never turned to look at the doctor as he moved slowly towards the door.

'I'm very sorry,' he said. 'It's a sad case. The drainage of this place is shameful. We positively invite disease. I can't do anything more. You can go on with the laudanum and the brandy; but I'm afraid it's useless. And you might put a mustard plaster to the soles of his feet.'

Mrs. Joyce sprang up and ran to the cupboard, as if awakened to new life. There was a ray of hope for her in being told to do something, even though in the same breath the doctor said that it was useless.

Cyril followed the doctor into the dusky alley. Summer stars were shining down upon them, through the dim gray night. Blotches of yellow light gleamed in wretched windows, where there were more rags than glass, and more paper than rags. Every door-step was occupied by squatting forms of slipshod matrons, or men in shirt sleeves, smoking their clay pipes. The fumes of rank tobacco contested for mastery with sulphuric acid and asafœtida. A horrible place to live in—a worse place to die in.

'Dr. Saunders, I would give a great deal to save that young man,' said Cyril, putting his arm through the doctor's. They had met continually during the troublous summer, and had grown very friendly.

'So would I, my dear sir,' answered Dr. Saunders. 'You don't suppose I'm adamant, do you? That woman's face has hit me harder than anything I've met with in the last miserable six weeks. But I can't help her. The young man is sinking.'

'Is not cholera more or less a disorganization of the blood?'

'Certainly.'

'Have you ever tried the effect of transfusion upon a patient in a state of collapse?'

'What do you mean?'

'When I was in Paris I heard a good deal about the transmission of blood from the veins of a healthy patient to those of a sinking one. I saw the operation performed at the Hôtel Dieu, and the result was successful.'

'That's an old idea,' said the parish doctor, 'but I've never gone into it. It was tried in the seventeenth century in France by Denis, the anatomist, and at Oxford by Dr. Richard Lower, who performed transfusion on animals. Dr. Blundell was the first

English physician who performed experiments of that kind on the human subject. I've never done such a thing myself, and I can't say I should like to attempt it.'

'It's the simplest process imaginable,' said Cyril, ' almost as easy as bleeding.'

And then he described the operation, as he had seen it performed in Paris.

'It may be easy enough, but I shouldn't care to try it.'

'Not to snatch a man from the jaws of death, not to achieve a triumph in medical science, not to prove how far this nineteenth century of ours is ahead of the learned Middle Ages, when the best cure surgery could invent for a sick emperor was to wrap him in the skin of an ape, flayed alive ?'

'Science is a grand thing,' admitted Dr. Saunders, ' but I am no friend to rash experiments. And even if I were willing to try the operation upon that poor fellow yonder—who is bound to die, so there's not much risk for *him*—where am I to find the benevolent subject willing to part with sufficient blood ?'

'Here,' answered Cyril. 'I am ready for your lancet.

CHAPTER XVIII.

'HAVE you thought of the danger to yourself?' asked the doctor, startled by Cyril's proposition.

'I do not care about the danger—if there be any.'

'There may be danger. You have been working night and day. You are by no means a patient I should consider able to lose several ounces of blood with impunity. You had better abandon the idea, Mr. Culverhouse. Your life is more valuable than that poor fellow's yonder.'

'I beg your pardon,' said Cyril. 'That young man is all the world to his widowed mother. I am all the world to nobody.'

'But you are valuable to a great number of people. Think how much good you have already done in this heathenish town. And you may go on being useful to your fellow-men for the next fifty years, if you do not waste your strength and health upon some benevolent folly.   Joyce is in the hands of Providence.   Medicine has done all that it can for him.'

'Medicine.   Yes—meaning drugs.   But science has done nothing.   I believe that science can save him.   Will you perform this operation, Mr. Saunders, yes or no ?'

'What if I say no ?'

' I shall go to every doctor in Bridford—down to the cattle doctors—till I find the man who will do it.'

'By the time you get to the end of your journey poor Joyce will have started for the other world.   But come, if you are absolutely bent upon this—stay, let me feel your pulse.   So strong and full.   Yes, I think we might risk it.   But you must have a cab ready at the end of the alley to take you home.   You will be weak and faint after the operation; and you will have to rest for an hour or so at Joyce's before we move you.'

'I'll go and order a cab while you go and get the instruments for the transfusion.   There is no time to be lost. If that poor fellow sinks into a state of collapse our efforts will be useless.'

Mr. Saunders went to his surgery, which was not far off, to fetch all that was required for the experiment. He was governed and impelled by a firmer spirit than his own, or he would hardly have done this thing.

' I ought not to do it on my own responsibility,' he said to himself. 'Suppose both men were to die, and there were an outcry against me in the newspapers. I should be ruined. If the air gets into the veins of either subject he is a dead man. I must have some one with me. Old Bolling would do. He's just the man. He would cut off a patient's head for the sake of an experiment, if the chances of his putting it on again properly were as one in fifty. He has killed more patients and made more wonderful cures than any doctor in the north of England.'

Fortunately Dr. Bolling's abode was not very remote. It was a shabby old square red brick house in the market-place, and had never been painted outside or inside within the memory of

man. It was a house of about twenty rooms. Old
Bolling lived in two of them, and his housekeeper
occupied a third. Rats, mice, spiders, beetles, and
such small deer had free warren in all the others.
There was a very fine breed of cockchafers on
which the old physician rather prided himself.
In the summer evenings they got into his lamp
and candles, and made his dingy old surgery musical. The furniture was a miracle of antiquity
and ugliness—tables as thick as tombstones—chairs
that only a strong man could move—horsehair
and moreen upholstery so interpenetrated with
dust that brushing or beating would have been a
mockery. Perhaps that is why the old housekeeper
never attempted either process.

Dr. Bolling seemed to have left off having
his windows cleaned at some early period of his
professional career. Perhaps the subdued light
which crept through his opaque and smoke-
darkened panes suited him, just as smoke-coloured
spectacles suit some people's eyes. The housekeeper had left off suggesting that the windows
would be better for cleaning.'

'What's the use?' Dr. Bolling had asked, years ago, when she hinted that the operation would improve the general appearance of his house. They'd get dirty again, wouldn't they?'

'Certainly,' agreed the housekeeper. 'They'd get dirty again—after a time.'

'Of course, and we should be no better off than we are now. I should have spent money on cleaning them for no purpose. Besides, if the windows were clean my old furniture might look shabby. Now in this tempered light, it looks uncommonly well.'

Common report declared that Dr. Bolling was a miser. The popular mind reasoned in this wise : that no man who was not a miser would live in one corner of a dirty old house, wear clothes too shabby for a Jew pedlar to chaffer for, and trot to and fro on his own feet from morning till night, when he could have afforded to make his house spick and span from basement to garret, clothe himself like a gentleman, and drive about in a handsome carriage and pair. But the actual fact was that Dr. Bolling did not

care about fine furniture or good broadcloth, and
that he liked to use his own legs better than to
sit behind a pair of horses. He was a creature
of habit. His mind was in his professional work.
He lived only for science. In the Middle Ages
he would have shut himself up in a laboratory
and made all manner of uncanny experiments, with
retorts and crucibles, and alembics, and much
waste of quicksilver. In our enlightened age
he confined his experiments to other people's
bodies. He was a marvel of cleverness, experience,
enthusiasm; but in Bridford he did not stand
nearly so high as Dr. Simper, who wore unexceptionable black, drove a smart brougham in winter,
and a smarter curricle in summer, and had his
shirts starched by a French laundress.

Lights were shining through the round holes
in Dr. Bolling's shutters when Mr. Saunders got
to his door.

'That's lucky,' thought the parish doctor. 'The
old man is in his surgery.'

He rang, and the door was opened by Dr. Bolling

himself, a shrivelled little man, with a black velvet skull-cap on the top of his bald head.

'Ah, Saunders, come in.   Anything wrong?

'A poor fellow dying of cholera, that's all.'

''That's bad.   I've tried everything—but though I've pulled a good many of my patients through, I'm not satisfied that I know much about the disease.   There must be a cure.   Every poison has its antidote.'

'Have you ever tried transfusion?'

'In cholera?   No.   I've done it in cases of severe hæmorrhage—and successfully.'

'I want you to do it to-night.'

And then the parish doctor told Dr. Bolling about Emmanuel Joyce and the curate's offer.

'Is your curate a strong man?'

'I should take him to be a healthy man.   He has been wasting his strength a good deal lately in attendance upon the sick.   But I should judge him to be a fair subject for the experiment.'

'We'll try it,' said the old man, his wizened face bright with energy and mind.   'I've known of its being tried in cholera cases.   It was done largely in Russia. Yes, I should like to see the effect. Cholera is a deterioration of the blood—and a supply of fresh healthy blood——Yes, I'll do it.'

There was no more time lost in discussion. Dr. Bolling went to one of the roomy old closets in his surgery, and fished out a particular form of syringe: armed with this and his instrument case he was ready.

The two doctors saw a cab waiting at the mouth of the alley, and they found Cyril Culverhouse standing in the doorway of the house that sheltered the Joyces. They all three went in together.

Two hours' later Cyril came out of that crowded den, very pale, and leaning on the parish doctor's arm. The two medical men had insisted upon his taking a glass of brandy, and reposing for some time in a horizontal position. The operation had been performed with every indication of success. Dr. Bolling was remaining to watch the patient. He was going to stay all night. Nobody knew better than Dr. Bolling's gratis patients whether or not the physician was a miser. He was no niggard either of his time or his money when their welfare was at stake. He would give as much attention to the case of a pauper infant— a little half-fledged life that was positively value- less from the political economist's point of view— as he would have given to a hypochondriacal duchess.

Mr. Saunders accompanied Cyril home to his lodgings, comfortable rooms in a queer old pan- elled house in a narrow street shadowed by the gloomy stone wall of the parish church. The rooms Cyril occupied were large, tidily furnished in an old-fashioned heterogeneous way, and scru- pulously clean. The landlady was what is usually called a motherly person, which seems to mean a woman whose easy temper has run into fat. She had let her lodgings to curates for the last thirty years, her husband, as parish clerk, having a vested right to church patronage. She was of a soft and affectionate nature, and, not being blessed with children of her own, lavished all her maternal feeling upon the beardless, or newly bearded youths who succeeded one another, in an endless procession, as occupants of her roomy first floor.

Lively curates had objected to the gloom of the dusky old panelled rooms, with their deep window-seats and narrow windows. Aristocratic curates had felt their personal dignity endangered by the shabbiness of this narrow side street ; but no curate had ever been able to resist the insinuations of Mrs. Podmore's maternal affection. They might complain, but they could not leave her. She shed tears at the least hint of such a desertion, and what curate, rightly minded, could resist a woman's tears ?

In her earlier life Mrs. Podmore had been able to ' do for' her curates, as she called it, with her own unassisted labour. She had cooked for them, and Mrs. Podmore's cookery was one of the charms by which she subjugated the clerical mind; she had kept their rooms clean and neat, and had even looked to their shirt buttons and darned their socks. But with advancing years and increasing obesity, Mrs. Podmore found herself compelled to take ' a girl,' and a series of neat-handed Phillises followed one

another in a line as long as Banquo's issue. Mrs
Podmore's requirements were high, and she demanded
an amount of virtue and industry from the genus girl
which very few specimens of that class were able to
maintain for more than a twelvemonth at a stretch.
Either the girl was saucy, and 'answered' when
Mrs. Podmore reproved her; or she was slovenly, and
left the flue in the corners of the rooms; or she was
that fearful animal, a breaker, and heralded her
approach by a crash of dropped crockery, or a shiver
of smashed glass.   For the period of her service,
however, Mrs. Podmore's girl was always neat and
pleasant to see. She was generally fresh-coloured,
and wore lavender gowns, with the sleeves rolled up
above the elbow, and her elbows as a rule were rosier
than Aurora's fingers.   To the curates she was rarely
saucy. They did not try her temper so severely as
Mrs. Podmore tried it.

In these quiet old-world lodgings Cyril Culver-
house awoke on the morning after the experiment.
The bells were ringing for the early morning service.
Cyril's usual hour for rising was full an hour earlier.
To-day it was only the sound of the bells close at

hand that awakened him. When he tried to lift his head from the pillow it was as heavy as lead.

' I'm afraid I'm going to be ill,' he thought.

He got up, took his cold bath, which revived him a little, struggled into his clothes, feeling weak and giddy and miserable all the while, and ran across to the church. The choir boys were filing into the chancel as he got to the vestry. The Vicar was looking glum.

' I say, Culverhouse, as this early service is your fad, you might at least be punctual,' he grumbled, as Cyril was pulling on his surplice.

' I'm sorry to be late, but I don't feel well this morning.'

' Eh ? Nothing bad, I hope. You're as white as your surplice. You go too much among those poor creatures. Very proper, of course ; but a man owes something to himself, even if he hasn't a wife and family to consider.'

Cyril got through his portion of the service somehow ; but the gray old church walls, the monuments to departed citizens, the draped females leaning upon anchors, the chubby cherubs blowing trumpets, the urns and tablets danced before his eyes, like a confused vision of a stonemason's yard turned upside down. He hardly knew what he was reading. His own voice had a far-away sound, as if it belonged to some one else, or were the echo of words he read yesterday. He had a curious uncertainty of mind about times and seasons, and could not have told whether it was winter or summer.

'I'm afraid I shall not be able to attend to my parish work this afternoon,' he said, when the service was over.

'No, no, my dear fellow,' answered the Vicar, heartily. 'Go home and rest. You've worked hard enough to have earned a few days' repose. I dare say that will set you right.'

Cyril went home, and threw himself down on his bed, and lay there helpless, inert, no one knowing anything about him, till Sarah, the maid-of-all-work, came at six o'clock to lay the table for his frugal dinner. Sitting-room and bedroom adjoined. Cyril had left the door open, and Sarah was startled at seeing him lying on his bed, dressed as he had come in from the church.

'I hope you are not ill, sir,' said Sarah.

Cyril gave her a rambling answer. She ran quickly down, and told Mrs. Podmore that Mr. Culverhouse had gone out of his mind. He was lying on his bed, and talking ever so queerly. The landlady waddled slowly upstairs, halting to pant at every landing, anxious, but too fat to travel fast, even if the house had been blazing. Just as she reached the first floor the street door bell rang. Sarah ran down to answer it, and found herself face to face with Dr. Saunders.

'Oh, sir, how lucky you've come!' exclaimed the girl, 'Mr. Culverhouse has gone out of his mind.'

'Nonsense, girl!'

The doctor ran upstairs and sat down by Cyril's bed. He found him very weak, and with a good deal of fever about him. He answered Dr. Saunders's questions with difficulty, and had a distressed and anxious look about his brow and eyes.

'I've some good news for you,' said the doctor, cheerily. 'Emmanuel Joyce rallied considerably during the night, and it's Bolling's opinion that he'll mend.'

'I'm very glad of that,' said Cyril, faintly.

'Now how about nursing?' inquired Mr. Saunders. 'This is a case of exhaustion and low fever. Mr. Culverhouse has been overworking himself lately, and he's thoroughly worn out. He will want a great deal of care. Good nursing will be important.'

'As far as my strength will let me he shall have every care,' protested Mrs. Podmore. 'But I can't boast of a strong constitution, and I'm troubled with my breath if I move about much. But as to beef . tea, and chicken broth, and jelly, I can make them as well as any one.'

'Beef tea and broth will be wanted; but the chief thing is to see that he takes them. He must have nourishment every half-hour. Look here, my good girl,' said Dr. Saunders, turning to the servant, 'you must help your mistress to nurse this gentleman day and night, till we can get a professional nurse.'

'Yes, sir,' said Sarah.

'I can make up a bed on the sitting-room sofa,' said Mrs. Podmore, 'so as to be always close at hand.'

'Yes, but that won't be much use if you're a heavy sleeper,' answered the doctor.

'I'm a very light sleeper, sir. I sometimes hear the church clock strike every hour of the night.'

'Living so near the belfry I hardly wonder that you do,' said the doctor.

He gave full directions as to what was to be done for his patient. It was not a case for drugs, but for care and nourishment. The loss of blood, coming upon a constitution much worn with work and watching, had caused a greater shock to the system than Dr. Saunders, or even Dr. Bolling, had apprehended.

In the next street the parish doctor ran against Mr. Pudge, a man with a pale fat face, greasy, smeared with printers' ink, sub-editor of the *Bridford Chronicle*.

'How are your patients going on?' asked Mr. Pudge. 'Any abatement of the epidemic?'

'None, I am sorry to say: but I've got a patient in Church Street that I'm more concerned about than all my cholera patients.'

'Who is that?'

'Mr. Culverhouse. He's down with fever. Overwork and anxiety have brought it on. He's been working as hard as that French bishop you've read about when the plague was raging at Marseilles.'

'Ay, to be sure,' said the sub-editor, who had never heard of the bishop or the plague at Marseilles, and who booked the fact as a good starting-point for his next leading article on the Bridford pestilence.

It was Friday afternoon, and Mr. Pudge was hastening to his office to see the *Chronicle* through the press. He did not forget to put in a paragraph, with a side heading,—

'SERIOUS ILLNESS OF THE REV. C. CULVERHOUSE. —We regret to hear that this gentleman, whose indefatigable labours among our suffering poor during the prevailing epidemic have been beyond all praise, has at length broken down under the burden imposed upon him, and is confined to his bed with a severe attack of fever.

CHAPTER XIX.

MR. PIPER FALLS IN LOVE.

ALL through the sultry summer weather Beatrix and
her companion, Madame Leonard, lived their quiet
lives at the Water House, with no change of scene
save to the wide airy moor, or to the hospitable
Vicarage, where they usually spent two or three
evenings of every week. People in Little Yafford,
except some bitter and envious spirits of the Coyle
type, had left off talking about Mr. Harefield's death,
and had begun even to feel somewhat ashamed of
their former suspicions about Beatrix. The girl's
calm front and resolute manner, her daily presence
among them, with that proud bearing which was
natural to her, gave the lie even to facts, where facts
were against her. If she had left the village, and
sought refuge from malevolent tongues in some
foreign country, Little Yafford would have been con-
firmed in its suspicions. She stayed, and the popular

voice for some time denounced her as bold and
brazen, hardened in wickedness, because she stayed ;
but by slow degrees this idea wore itself out.   Her
steadiness outwore suspicion, as water wears rock.

Every month, and sometimes every mail, brought
Beatrix an Indian letter.   Her lover sent her a full
account of his life, which had now become full of
action and excitement.   The second Burmese war
had broken out, and was being carried on with more
valour than discretion.   A town was taken trium-
phantly and with little loss, and then abandoned to
the care of a force too weak to keep or defend it.
Retaken by the enemy, it had to be conquered again,
and this time with a severe struggle.   Prome was
taken twice ; the city of Pegu three times.   Detach-
ments were cut off ; officers were murdered.

Sir Kenrick's regiment was in the thick of the
strife.   He had won his captaincy, and hoped, in
a struggle that favoured rapid promotion, to get
another step before he came home.

'I wonder if you will think better of me, Beatrix,'
he wrote, 'if I come back a major ?   There is a
middle-aged sound about the title that you might

hardly appreciate; but I assure you it is rather a
grand thing now-a-days for a man to be a major
before he is thirty. We are having a very jolly time
of it—plenty of fighting—a state of things that I
have always longed for. I felt myself born too late
in being out of the Sikh war, when I heard our
fellows disputing over their claret about Mooltan and
Goojerat. But now I have had my chance, like the
rest, and I hope that we may have peace before
Christmas, so that I may see your dear face by
the time the crocuses are golden in the Vicarage
garden.'

Then came a spirited description of the last skir-
mish. Beatrix followed the news of the war with
attention and anxiety. She sometimes felt that her
heart was wickedly calm in this period of danger and
uncertainty. Any mail might bring the news of her
lover's death, cut down from a scaling-ladder, or
treacherously murdered by the foe. Every letter she
received might be the last that strong young hand
would pen. Though Kenrick wrote so lightly and
gaily of the war, the facts were not less awful. It
was an insignificant business in the history of the

world, perhaps, but death was as busy there as at Marathon or Waterloo.

'If I loved him as I ought to love my betrothed husband, I should not have a moment's peace,' Beatrix thought, full of self-reproach.

Towards the close of the summer, just at the time when Emmanuel Joyce was stricken with cholera, Beatrix's health began to languish a little, and at Mr. Namby's advice she went to Whitby with Madame Leonard, intending to remain away some weeks.

It was about this time that Bella Scratchell's life became full of perplexity and excitement. A curious, most unlooked-for event had happened, and had changed the whole colour of the Scratchell existence. Mr. Scratchell declared that Providence, pleased with the Scratchells' industry, economy, and patience, had at length taken the family under its wing, as directly and obviously as the Jews were taken in hand by the Divine power in the time of Moses. Mr. Scratchell did not absolutely expect that miracles were to be worked for him, that waters were to be turned into blood, or flies to swarm in kings' chambers;

but, short of this, he considered himself a very proper subject for Divine favour.

Mr. Piper had fallen in love with Bella, and wished to make her the second Mrs. Piper.

Like most men who mourn a first wife with a somewhat exaggerated dolefulness, Mr. Piper had speedily discovered a yearning to take to himself a second. He had not far to look for this second choice. Bella had always appeared to his taste as the prettiest thing he knew. Her round plump beauty, the sunny tints of her hair, her peachy cheeks, and red full lips, her dimples and small round chin, her little white hands and neatly shaped feet, all were after the fashion which in Mr. Piper's eye seemed the perfection of womanly beauty. A strong-minded woman, beautiful as Venus and grand as Juno, would have had no attraction for him. Mr. Piper had an awful dread of being hen-pecked. He wanted a wife whom he could treat kindly, and govern with a rod of iron. That rod of iron would be nicely swathed in cotton-wool and velvet, of course, but it would be unbending. Mr. Piper had enjoyed life in his own way for the last twenty years, and he meant to go on having his own way so long as his faculties remained to him. Short of being like Dean Swift, and dying 'first a'top,' Mr. Piper meant to have his own way, until he drew his last breath.

Bella appeared to him by far the most pliable and soft-hearted young woman of his acquaintance, as well as the prettiest. His children did not like her, but that was natural. The young Pipers had so strong a bent towards ignorance that they would have hated any one who tried to teach them. Mr. Piper was not going to be governed by his children's prejudices. The very best thing he could do for them would be to give them such a step-mother as Bella. The girls were wild, rough, and tomboyish. Constant intercourse with a well-mannered young woman would tone them down.

'She's every inch the lady,' Mr. Piper said to himself, 'and she'll make ladies of my gals, if they'll let her.'

Bella had long been conscious of a lurking gallantry in Mr. Piper's manners, which made that worthy little man odious to her. She had avoided him as much as possible, hurrying out of the dull handsome house directly the formal hours of study were over. She had absolutely refused all his invitations to luncheon, despite his reproachful assertion that she was wanting in compassion for his widowed and lonely state.

'You have your daughters for companions, Mr. Piper,' she replied to those charges. 'You can't want me.'

'But I do,' retorted Mr. Piper. 'My gals are no company for me. They haven't mind enough, and they're not pretty enough. I like to see a pretty face on the other side of the table, when I sit down to my victuals.'

Bella shuddered. Could any girl—even one who had known poverty's sharp stings from her cradle upwards—consent to marry a man who talked about victuals? There was no harm in the word; it was neither obscene nor blasphemous, but it was revolting.

Although reproachful, Mr. Piper was not vindictive. The spring and summer that followed poor Mrs. Piper's death were seasons of fatness

and plenty for the Scratchell family. Mr. Piper
was always sending Mrs. Scratchell some offering
from his model farm. Cream, butter, poultry, vege-
tables, the first fruits of the season, forced into
premature being at much cost of money and
labour, came to the Scratchell door in delicious
succession. The young Scratchells grew epicurean,
and turned up their noses at rhubarb pudding
with a crust two inches thick. They wanted early
gooseberries, tasting of the wood. Mr. Piper's
servants—who stopped longer in his service now
that the careful housewife was gone—had a good
deal to say about these small gifts. It was evident which way the wind was setting. Miss
Scratchell would soon be mistress of the Park.

'There will be a second Mrs. Piper before
Christmas, or else my name ain't Martha Blair,'
said the cook. 'And Miss Scratchell will be the
party.'

'Well,' sighed the housemaid, without looking
up from her stocking-darning, 'if he's bent on marrying he may as well marry her as any one else.
She's haffable and heven-tempered, I should think.'

'Should you?' inquired the cook, ironically. 'That shows 'ow much *you* knows about 'ooman natur. That young woman is deeper than the deepest well that was ever dug, and if ever she's missus here she'll want to rule everythink with a 'igh 'and. Them mealy-mouthed ones always do. I'd rather 'ave a spit-fire for a missus than one of them soft-spoken young women that go smilin' through the world as if they was apologizin' to everybody for bein' alive. She'll spend 'is money and she'll break 'is 'art, and she'll use all of us like dogs. That's my opinion about Miss Scratchell, if you wish to know it.'

'Lor', cook! you're such a one to jump at conclusions,' said the housemaid, with a somewhat contemptuous shrug.

'Perhaps I am, Mary; but I generally jumps at 'em right.'

CHAPTER XX.

ONE August morning, just about the time of Cyril's illness, Bella Scratchell found her pupils a shade more averse from the delights of learning, and generally unpleasant in their behaviour, than usual. The morning was sultry, there was thunder in the air, and some of the thunder seemed to have got into the young Pipers, who were as dull and leaden as the sky, and as sulkily silent as the heavy-headed limes on the lawn, whose branches flopped moodily, with never a rustle of leaf or a whisper among the boughs.

Then all at once the young Pipers—moved to rebellion by the imposition of a task which seemed too much for their feeble minds — broke into murmurs and grumblings, what time the trees began to rustle and shiver, and talk to one another mysteriously about the fast coming storm, while the birds set up scared twitterings, and chattered of impending peril and desolation.

Presently came great drops spattering upon the iron verandah outside the schoolroom window — harbingers of a flood — and then the rain came down in a dense sheet of water, and the lightning flashed pale and sickly illumination over the gray rain-blotted landscape, and the thunder roared awfully, like some infuriated giant threatening Little Yafford, from his lurking-place in a cleft of the hills.

The young Pipers gave vent to their terror in shrill screams and yappings, and cowered in corners, with their heads shrouded in their pinafores. They were terrified at the storm, but they were glad of its coming, since it afforded an excellent excuse for avoiding their lessons.

'You can't expect us to say French verbs in a thunderstorm,' remonstrated Elizabeth Fry, when Bella tried to continue her course of instruction. 'The subjunctive's difficult enough at the best of times,—a lot of ridiculous words ending in *issc*— but it's a little too bad with the lightning glaring in one's face.'

'I shouldn't wonder if ma had asked for this storm on purpose to frighten *you*,' said Brougham, addressing himself vindictively to his governess. 'She's in heaven, you know, and can see how badly you treat us.'

Bella abandoned the lessons as hopeless. She could not go home in this flood of rain. She stood at the window, watching the storm, while her pupils, released from the thraldom of study, and grown hardened to the tempest, rioted about the room, knocked over the chairs, pelted each other with lesson books, and concluded every argument with fisticuffs. She did not attempt to check this youthful exuberance—first, because she knew any such endeavour would be worse than useless; and secondly, because the supervision of her pupils' moral conduct was not in the bond. She was engaged and paid to teach them a smattering of various languages, history, grammar, geography, and to superintend their musical studies in the absence of the professor. Nothing more.

At one o'clock the rain had ceased and the storm had abated, though the sky still looked heavy. One o'clock was Bella's hour for leaving her pupils ; half-past one was their hour for dinner. The half-hour between one o'clock and dinner-time was a period of peculiar strife and riot, the evil tempers of the youthful Pipers being exacerbated by hunger. There was always a warm conflict between them and the young woman told off for their service, who wanted them to have 'their 'ands washed and their 'air brushed for dinner,' and who was threatened with Mr. Piper's condign displeasure if she sent them into the dining-room unkempt and uncleaned.

In Mrs. Piper's lifetime Bella had generally aided in this struggle, but she was now in the habit of going away directly the lessons were over.

On this particular occasion she found Mr. Piper smoking his cigar in the hall, as she had found him very often lately. Hitherto she had contrived to slip by him with a friendly good morning, or at most a brief interchange of remarks about the weather, and a grateful little speech in acknowledgment of his last offering from the farm or the kitchen-garden. To-day she could not escape so easily.

'You ain't agoin' yet, Beller,' said Mr. Piper, laying his stumpy fingers on her arm. 'Look at that there sky! It 'll rain 'eavens 'ard presently.'

'Then I had better get home before it begins,' suggested Bella.

'No, you don't. I'm not going to be avoided in this way. Widowers ain't poison, that a young woman need shun them as if her life was in danger. I want to have a serious talk with you, Beller. I've been wanting such a talk for a long time, but you've managed to give me the slip. This day I'm determined to say my say. You ain't going out under that sky, and you are going to hear what I've got to tell you. That's how it's going to be.'

'You have such strength of will, Mr. Piper,' said Bella, with her pretty laugh. 'How could a poor little thing like me oppose you?'

'You ain't a poor little thing,' retorted Mr. Piper. 'You're a pretty little thing, and you ain't poor. No young woman with your attractions can be poor. There's always some one in the background ready to lay his 'art and 'and at her feet.'

· Bella shuddered. Mr. Piper's conversation was growing significant. She would have given a great deal to get away. She thought of Cyril Culverhouse, of one who in her mind was the image of dignity and refinement. What would his love have been like, could she have won it? In what sweet words, borrowed unconsciously from divinest poet, would he have whispered his passion? And here was Mr. Piper breathing hard, and looking odiously warm and puffy, evidently bent upon making her an offer.

'And, if he should ask me, all of them at home would want me to accept him,' thought Bella, despairingly. 'I should be worried to death.'

'Come into the drawing-room,' said Mr. Piper. 'The children won't interrupt us there. I want to be serious.'

He led her into that rarely used apartment, which had a vault-like aspect now that Mrs. Piper no longer recived her morning visitors in it. She had been wont to regale her guests in a stately manner with sherry and fancy biscuits, brought in upon a monster salver, of the Prince Regent's period, in Garrard's worst style, with massive gadroon edges and a great flourish of engraving, as weighty as a coal-scuttle. The room had smelt of sherry and biscuits in Mrs. Piper's time. Now it only smelt of mildew.

There was a centre ottoman under the chandelier, a birthday present from Mr. Piper to his wife, and one of the first of its kind that had been seen in Little Yafford. Upon this the manufacturer seated himself, with his shoulder at an uncomfortable angle with Bella's shoulder, after the manner of such ottomans.

'Bella, I've been in love with you ever so long,' exclaimed Mr. Piper, plunging desperately into the middle of things.

'Good gracious, Mr. Piper, how can you say anything so horrible?' cried Bella. 'Your poor dear wife has been dead hardly six months.'

'I was not in love with you during my sainted wife's lifetime,' said Mr. Piper. 'My principles are too firmly fixed for that. I am not a Mahomedan. But I had an eye for the Beautiful, even in Mrs. Piper's lifetime, and I knew that you came up to the mark in that line. Mrs. Piper's death left a vide here.' Mr. Piper touched his waistcoat, to indicate that the vacuum was in his heart. 'A vide which I feel you can fill. You can be a refined and ladylike mother to my children, a clever mistress of my house, and a comfort and happiness to me. It is in you to be all that, Bella, I know it and feel it; and I will go so far as to say that it is a fine opportunity for you—an opportunity which any young woman in your position would be proud to grasp.'

'I could never marry where I did not love,' faltered Bella, foreseeing no end to the trouble at home that would come out of this.

'Perhaps not,' said Mr. Piper, looking warmer and puffier than ever, 'but what's to prevent your loving me?'

'I respect you,' murmured Bella, feeling obliged to say something civil.

'Well, that's halfway,' answered the widower, with a satisfied air. 'You begin with respect, you'll get on to love before you know where you are. I'm proud to say I've always made myself respected

everywhere. I've kept my sack upright. Twenty
shillings in the pound has been my guiding star.
Go on respecting me, Bella. You'll wake up some
morning and find that respect has blossomed into
love.'

Here Mr. Piper put his arm round Bella's
waist. She found that it would not do to tem-
porize.

'Dear Mr. Piper,' she said, putting on that
pretty beseeching manner which stood in such good
stead with her on most occasions, ' you are all
that is kind and generous, but indeed it can
never be.'

' What can never be ? '

'I can never be your wife. I will not speak
of the disparity in our ages, because——'

'Because that's rubbish,' interrupted the im-
patient Piper. ' You'd better be an old man's
darling than a young man's slave. I know what
the young men of the present day are. Between
you and I and the post they're an uncommon bad
lot. You'd better think twice before you refuse
such an offer as mine, Beller. It 'isn't every pretty

girl that gets such a chance once in her life. Don't
you expect to get it twice. Just you think who
it is you're refusing. I could buy up everybody
for ten miles round Little Yafford. I'm not a man
to boast of the money I've made. Everybody
knows what I am at Great Yafford—and further
afield. My name on the back of a bill is as good
as the Bank of England. Look at this place. I
could buy it to-morrow, if I liked—and if you say
"buy it, Piper," I'll buy it, and place you as 'igh
as any of the old county famblies. Sir Philip
Dulcimer don't care for the place. It's me that
has made it what it is. Look at the furniture and
ornaments I've bought, to please poor Mrs. Piper—
this very ottermon we're sitting on, five-and-thirty
pound, the newest thing out. You'd better think
twice—and a good many times twice—before you
turn up your nose at such an offer as mine. I'll
allow you three hundred a year for dress and fallals.
Yes—settle it upon you in black and white—and
that's a deal more than ever I did for poor Moggie.
She had to ask me for a ten-pound note when she
wanted it.'

Bella gave a faint shiver. Three hundred a
year for pocket-money! What fabulous wealth it
seemed! But three hundred a year with Mr. Piper
—to have that warm puffiness, that blustering vul-
garity, always in attendance upon her—to be called
Beller all her life—to see across the domestic
hearth that odious figure of low-born merit and
commercial prosperity! No, it would be too dreadful. She could not bear it. She was fond of
money—nay, she loved it with the ravenous love that
often comes of a poverty-stricken youth. If she
had never known Cyril Culverhouse—never set her
affections on that high type of manhood—she might,
perhaps, have brought herself to tolerate Mr. Piper,
for the sake of Little Yafford Park and unlimited
drapery. But now—oh! it was impossible.

She looked round the drawing-room. It was
spacious and lofty, but eminently commonplace
in all its details. She began to think, idly—while
the widower sank into a stertorous reverie, with his
hands plunged deep into his shepherd's plaid
pockets—how she would make Mr. Piper refurnish
the room if she were his wife. All those clumsy

rosevood chairs and tables should be turned out,
to give place to light gilded furniture, of the Louis
Seize period, upholstered with sky-blue satin. The
revival of old Dutch taste had not yet set in.
People had not begun to go mad about Queen Anne
cabinets and blue and white ginger-jars. Bella's
imagination did not soar above gilded chairs and
blue satin curtains.

'Come,' said Mr. Piper, shaking himself out of
his abstraction, like a dog coming out of the water,
'come, Beller, what's your ultamatum? Yes or no?'

'No,' said Bella, firmly. 'I am sorry to seem
ungrateful for your flattering regard, but I can only
answer no.'

And then she glanced round the drawing-room
again, and thought how pretty it would look, all
gy with blue and gold, and what a grand thing it
would be to sit there, elegantly dressed, framed in
fowers, like an old portrait by Boucher, receiving
te best people in Little Yafford, and patronizing
Iiss Coyle.

'Well, I'm sorry,' said Mr. Piper, in his matter-
f-fact tone, 'and I think you're a fool. Excuse

me for mentioning it, but that's my opinion, and I'm a man that always speaks my mind.'

'Perhaps, under the circumstances, it might be better for me not to come here any more,' suggested Bella, rising to depart.

'Well, I don't know. It might be rather aggravating to my feelings for me to see you, perhaps—but never mind me. I'm nobody.'

'I am sure I had better not come,' said Bella. 'You will easily find some one to replace me.'

'Oh, Lord, yes,' exclaimed Mr. Piper, tesily. 'Governesses are as plentiful as blackberries. Old and ugly, most of em—the cleverer they are the uglier. And bony. I find that learning generally runs into bone. If ever I see a man whose elbow and knee joints stand out extra sharp, and whose hair hasn't been made acquainted with a pair of scissors for a twelvemonth, I make up my mind that he's a professor.'

'Good-bye,' faltered Bella, holding out her hand. 'I hope you don't feel angry with me?'

'I don't feel pleased with you,' answered Mr. Piper, 'and I'm too candid to pretend it. Good-by'

They shook hands, and Bella went home, feeling very uncomfortable. She had refused the richest man in the neighbourhood, and she had lost her situation. How would the intelligence of these two facts be received by her anxious mother and her stony-hearted father? Bella knew that she would have to endure the reproaches and upbraidings of both.

CHAPTER XXI.

CYRIL'S NURSES.

WHILE the church bells were ringing daily in the tower above his head, and the old Bridford chimes, famous long ago, were heralding the birth of every hour with a fine old psalm tune that pealed out over the busy, money-making city, like an echo of the past, Cyril Culverhouse was lying at the bottom of a dark gulf of pain and confusion, and all the outer world, and all the life that he had lived, were cancelled and forgotten.

Strange images danced before his eyes like motes in the sunshine, yet seemed to him neither strange nor unexpected. He had a history of his own in that period of delirium, a new identity, new surroundings, a mad, wild world, peopled out of his own brain. Bishops and archbishops came and sat beside his bed, and held long arguments with him, figments of a mind distraught, the shadows that haunt fever-dreams, but to him intensely real. The dead came back to life to hold converse with him, and he was not surprised. No, he had always thought there was something in the ideas of the old necromancers. The elixir of life was not an impossibility. Here was Luther with his square solid face, and sensual humorous mouth. Here was Pascal, full of quaint sayings and far-reaching thoughts. The sick man talked for all of them. His talk was wildest raving to the ears that listened, but to his own fancy it was profoundest wisdom. There is no egotism, no belief in self, equal to that of the lunatic. For him the stars and moon have been made, for him God willingly performs miracles which overthrow all the laws of the universe. He is the axis of the world, and lets it go round.

How long those days and nights of fever were! That was the chief agony of them. The eternity of hours, so thickly peopled with distorted shapes that every quarter of an hour was an era. Of actual physical pain the sufferer had no consciousness; but weariness, almost too heavy to be borne weighed upon him in the long strange nights, when the faces of his watchers changed, and the very walls of his room seemed new and unknown to him. He fancied that his nurses had removed him into new lodgings while he slept, though it seemed to him that he had never slept.

Sometimes he fancied himself in one place, sometimes in another. He was at Oxford, in those old rooms of his looking into the college garden. He was at Little Yafford, at Culverhouse, anywhere but where he really was.

And his nurses, who were they? He faintly remembered Mrs. Podmore leaning over his bed, fat and scant of breath, with a medicine-glass in her hand, coaxing him to drink. He remembered Sarah, making believe to step softly, in creaking shoes, whose every movement was agony to him. But these things were lost in the darkness of remote ages. His present nurses seemed to have been tending him during a century.

There were two, one tall and slender, dignified of bearing, yet gracious in every movement; the other short, small, and brisk. They were dressed

exactly alike, in the costume of some religious
order, as he supposed. They wore long black
robes and white linen caps, such as he remembered to have seen worn by the Sisters of Mercy
in Breton towns that he had visited years ago in
one of his long vacations. Admirable caps for
ugly women, for the stiff linen borders projected
a quarter of a yard beyond the face, entirely concealed the profile, and overshadowed the countenance at all times.

Cyril knew only that the taller of his two
nurses had dark eyes and a pale face, and that
the little woman had black eyes of exceeding
sharpness, that flashed at him from the cavernous
cap. They were both admirable nurses, quiet,
gentle, attentive, but in some phases of his delirium he hated them, and accused them of all
manner of evil designs. They were poisoning
him. Yes, the medicine they made him take at
stated intervals contained a slow poison—the *Aqua
Tofana* of the Middle Ages—that horrible stuff
which the wicked witch Toffania made by whole-
sale, and sent to all the cities of the earth as the

manna of St. Nicola of Bari ; or it was the hem-
lock that Socrates drank, or wolf's bane, or deadly
nightshade.   He recognised the flavour of the
murderous herb.'   And then he stormed at his
nurses, and told them they had plotted his murder.

'If you were honest women you would not
hide your faces,' he cried.   'You are murderesses,
and have come here to kill me.'

One night, after an age of fever and hallu-
cination, he sank into a refreshing slumber.   It
was as if his spirit, newly escaped from a burning
hell, had slipped unawares into Paradise.   Fair
meadows and flowing streams, an ineffable sense
of coolness and relief, and then deep rest and
stillness.

When he awoke, the summer dawn filled the
room.   Through the widely opened windows came
the fresh breezes of the morning.   A soft cool
hand was on his brow, the tall nurse's dark figure
stood beside his bed.

All his delusions, all his hideous fancies, seemed
to have run out of his brain, like water out of a
sieve, during that one sweet sleep. ·Suddenly and

completely as the leper at the Divine Healer's
bidding, he was made sound and whole. Very
weak still, with a sense of utter helplessness and
prostration, he yet felt himself cured. The fire
that had made life a torture had burnt itself out.

He looked up at his nurse. How purely white
that quaint old head-gear of hers looked in the
morning sunshine. He remembered the bright
freshness of just such another morning in his
holiday rambles five years ago, and just such
another black-robed figure and white cap, a Sister
of Mercy waiting for the starting of the diligence,
in the old market square at Vannes, the white
dusty square, the scanty trees, that seem to have
been planted yesterday, the shabby old cathedral
looking down at him.

'You are a Frenchwoman, are you not?' he
asked, the weakness of his voice startling him a little.

'*Mais si*,' she answered, gently.

He tried to get her to talk, but she answered
him only in monosyllables. He tried to see her face,
but the position in which she held her head always
prevented him.

'Perhaps her cap is the prettiest thing about her,
and she would rather show that than her face,' he
thought.

Even that brief conversation exhausted him, and
he fell asleep again. Those weary hours of delirious
wakefulness had left him long arrears of sleep to
make up. He slept on till dusk, and Dr. Saunders,
finding him locked in that deep slumber, pronounced
him out of danger.

'Our medicines have never been able to touch
him,' he said frankly. 'It has been an unaided
struggle between nature and disease. I ought not to
say unaided, though,' he added, apologetically, to the
little nursing sister in the Breton cap. 'Your care
has been a very powerful assistance.

The little woman thanked him effusively in her
broken English. The taller nurse spoke only French,
and as little of that as possible.

When Cyril awoke again, just before nightfall,
the small nurse was sitting by his bed.

'Where is the other ?' he asked.

'Gone.'

'Gone ? '

'Yes. You are now much better—on the high road to recovery. You no longer want two nurses. My companion has gone home.'

'She is wanted for some other case, perhaps.'

'No doubt she soon will be.'

To what order do you belong ?'

'To a community of nursing sisters.'

'In Brittany ?'

'Yes.'

'What part of Brittany ?'

'We never talk about ourselves. It is one of the rules of our order. We come and go like the wind.'

'But how was it that you came to me ? Who sent for you ?'

'We were not sent for. We happened to hear of your illness—and we knew you were a good man. It was our duty to come and nurse you.'

'What me ?—a Protestant ?'

'We are not sectarian. We go wherever we are wanted.'

'But how do you—Breton nuns—come to be in England ?'

'We are not nuns. We are a nursing sisterhood, bound by no vows. We heard of the pest raging in this town, and came here to be useful.'

'You are very good people,' said Cyril. 'I am sorry the other sister is gone. I should like to have talked to her, but this morning she would answer me only in monosyllables.'

'It is not good for you to talk, and it is one of our rules to talk as little as possible.'

For three days the figure in the loose black gown was constantly at Cyril's bedside. He heard the little woman telling her beads in the dead of night. If she were no nun she was at any rate a staunch Roman Catholic; but she did not endeavour to convert him to her own creed. She was a modest, unobtrusive little woman; but during those three days she very often broke the rule of her order, and talked to the patient a good deal. She talked of Brittany, which she knew thoroughly, and sometimes of modern French literature, which she knew better than she ought to have done as a member of a religious sisterhood.

On the fourth day she was gone, and another

figure, dressed in black, with neat white cap and apron, was by Cyril's bedside. The face of this watcher was not hidden. He knew it well, a homely English face that brought back the thought of his work in the courts and back streets of Bridford.

'Mrs. Joyce,' he exclaimed. 'Have you turned nurse?'

'What more blessed privilege can I have, sir, than to take care of you? I owe you what is a great deal more to me than my own life, the life of my beloved son. Oh, sir, if he ever comes to be a Milton or a Shakespeare, the world will bless you for your goodness, as I do now.'

Cyril smiled at her enthusiasm. Perhaps every mother whose son writes obscure verses in doubtful English believes with Mrs. Joyce that she has produced a Milton.

'I should have come before, sir, if the two ladies hadn't been here. But they were such good nurses I didn't want to interfere with them.'

'Do you know where they came from, or why they came?'

'No, indeed, Mr. Culverhouse. They were

foreigners, and I suppose they came from foreign parts.'

'Neither of my doctors sent for them, I believe.'

'No, sir. Dr. Saunders told me they came and went like spirits, but he was wishful there were more like them.'

'And your son is really recovered?'

'Yes, sir. It is a most wonderful cure. He rallied that night, and was up and about at the end of the week. To both of us it seemed like a miracle. I have read the gospel about the widow's son every night and morning after my prayers, and I have read it two or three times to Emmanuel. Oh, sir, I hope and believe you have wrought a double cure. I think my son's heart is turned to holy things. He has read his Bible very often lately. I have watched him, and I think he is beginning to find out that there is truth and comfort to be found in it.'

'He cannot read the gospel long without making that discovery. Young men are too apt to form their judgment of the Bible from what other people have written about it. When they go to the fountain head they find their mistake.'

Cyril was not satisfied till he had questioned Dr. Saunders and Dr. Bolling, the latter of whom had come to see him daily, without any fee, about the two French nurses. But neither of these could tell him more than he knew already.

'I wish I did know more about them,' said Mr. Saunders. 'Whatever institution they belong to, it's an admirable one, and I'm sorry we haven't a few more institutions of that kind over here. I don't think we should have pulled you through if it hadn't been for that excellent nursing. No, upon my word I believe you owe those two women your life.'

'And I do not even know their names, or where they are to be found,' said Cyril, regretfully.

It worried him not a little to be under so deep an obligation, and to have no mode of expressing his gratitude. At one time he thought of putting an advertisement in the *Times*, thanking his unknown nurses for their care. But on reflection this seemed idle. They were doubtless what they represented themselves, sisters of some religious order, who did good for the love of God. They had no need of his thanks. Yet he puzzled himself not a little about the whole business. Why should he have been selected, above all other sufferers in the town of Bridford, as the recipient of this gratuitous care?

As soon as he was able to leave his bed, Dr. Bolling insisted on his going off to the sea-side to get strength before he went back to his work. This vexed him sorely, but he could not disobey.

'You've been as near the gates of death as a man can well go without passing through them,' said the doctor.

END OF VOL. II.

J. AND W. RIDER, PRINTERS, LONDON.